Root Cause

Garden of Unearthly Delights, Part II

By

Steven Dunne

Prologue

They left me there for dead in that swamp, the bastards. Must've been hundreds of miles from where I was picked up. I'm not even sure where there could even be swampland in this area. Was I drugged? Hit on the head? Things weren't adding up.

Everything smelled the way I imagined quicksand from old TV shows like Gilligan's Island would. Like stale bread and a beach after the rain. Not that clean rain scent bullshit they try to sell you at the mall, the rain that washed fish carcases up on the shore.

While I perseverated on the smell and how it enacted my childhood nightmare of falling into a pit of quicksand (which would top my list of never had I ever moments) I was slowly drifting downward into a pit of quicksand. Not really quicksand so much. It was a bog. And my hands and feet were tied.

The last thing I remember from that night was seeing a blue '87 Honda Civic hatchback roll up into the parking lot of the bar I was at, the Strick 9. It was the best spot in Old Town Vegas to get your freak on, provided you liked old school post-punk and didn't mind fairies. Not that kind. The kind that cast spells on forests and make you think you've switched bodies with your dog: The Fey.

The club was a known Haven for the fair folk. That was part of it's charm for me. I went outside for a smoke and to get some non-enchanted air when the Civic rolled up. I thought to myself how long it's been since I saw a Honda Civic hatchback when I felt a jab in my neck and everything went dark. I woke up chest deep in muck.

I felt myself start to sink deeper. I knew the key to getting out of this was maintaining a sense of balance and calm but fuck if that isn't made difficult by the notion of suffocation. Back when I wore my old hat, as Sorcerer Supreme, this would've been a non-issue. I probably would never have been jumped by those clowns.

My eyes strained against the darkness. My senses were turning on me, making clear the unseeable and garbage of the visible. Somewhere in the midst of the physical exhaustion, the tranquilizers, and the inhalation of swamp gas, I was losing it. What little I could make out wasn't making much sense, even for one as accustomed to mystical experiences as myself. The swamp was gathering itself into a loose conglomeration of a roughly humanoid form. As the clouds passed over, the intermittent glinting moonlight made swaths of slow strobing across the plant-human form. As the light came and went, I could swear I could see it moving, writhing. Ever so painfully slowly moving in undulating thrusts toward me as I lay there, trapped in the mire.

Closer it crept. Initially I was terrified. When I was a Master of the Mystic arts, this would have been no match for my might. I would have dispatched the thing and went on about my business. Being but a mortal man, I was at a loss. I opened my mouth to scream, but all that escaped was the steely din of silence. The screams had fallen to the mindless panic. I felt my head growing lighter and the corners of my vision darker. Until there was nothing but darkness and I wrapped in it until slipping from consciousness.

I woke with a start, the creature still several feet away. At this point, my abject terror had given way to questioning boredom. Really? I understand the creeping doom vibe, but this had taken things to a whole new level of stupid. There comes a time when the dragging of the blade across stone goes from being maddeningly terrifying to desensitizing. I think it just took me this long to remember who I was.

"Look. I'm Neil Fucking Hawthorne. Unless you want to be ready for a bad fucking day, I recommend you give me some of that foliage and help me out of this pit. Otherwise, I'm gonna figure out a way to break that bramble off and shove it up your ass." I announced.

The creature ceased advancing. I wasn't entirely sure what was happening. It seemed as if my bravado was all that was necessary to avoid my destruction at the tiny thorny hands of vegetative vengeance.

"So. What's it gonna be?" I yelled.

"Neil?" I heard a voice call from inside the mass. It was familiar. *Where did I know that voice?*

"Alan?" I said with a query. "Dr. Alan Scott?"

The plant creature stood up erect. "In the flesh." It beamed, and extended a tendril to hoist me out of the quicksand. I was returned safely to terra firma and Alan motioned me to follow him. "Let's go have a spot of tea and catch up on old times." He bellowed.

This is not the weirdest day I've had, but pretty fucking close.

We sat, had a cup of tea, and talked about what he had been up to since working in Resistance. Turns out he figured out how to turn himself into plant life. Go figure. Once the hallucinogens wore off, I was sitting in Strick-9 again. Not willing to delve too deeply into what, if anything had actually transpired.

I took a sip of the drink in front of me. It was Earl Grey. Lukewarm. Ah yes, another day in paradise.

Chapter 1: This Desert Life

Las Vegas takes a toll on a man. Twelve months of artificial sunlight, Elvis impersonators, and dead-eyed lost souls walking the streets starts to build up gunk in a person's psyche. When I was acting as the Sorcerer Supreme, I came into contact with all kinds of nastiness but I had a barrier between myself and the world around me. I had tools, I had vestments. Ever since I was removed from my post, I've been nothing but a bare wire. I've helped where I could, but found that I was of little good in a place that was determined to maintain an aire of living death.

The main task of being a Necromancer is moving the universal wheel. We transition souls from one stage to another, be it life into death, death into the next life, or within stages of a life. This place is committed and determined to keep people stuck in a moment. Las Vegas is the human equivalent to flypaper. It is a life sucking vortex from which there is no escape.

That being said, I had no plans of leaving. I had met the closest thing my coal black heart could equate to love. She and I have been living together since I moved out here from New Orleans. I say live with in the same manner as anyone can really live with someone who is Dark Fae.

Live with is kind of an oversell. We walk parallel paths. Sometimes those paths intersect, but by and large we each do our own thing.

I've been whoring myself out as a private detective with the goal of finding lost people. Most of what I found were dead leads. Occasionally a dead person. I am comfortable with Death, but the death is not the tragedy. The tragedy lies in the debt that is paid by the living. Where the deceased has completed their transition (most of the time) more times than not, the living keep walking their road without full realization that they need to let go of their lost loved one. Not only for their own mental health, but each one of those attachments is a chord that ties the departed back to the world of the Living. Do you want to get ghosts? That's how you get ghosts.

I've been living with my partner for the last year or so and I still don't know her name. I have a name I call her, but I know damn well that isn't her real name. She tried to tell me her name once, I shut that down with the quickness. With all we had been through, I didn't want to cheapen it with her having to owe me anything. Good standard operating practice is never tell a magician your true name. If they really want to find it out, they can in other ways. You telling the magician your name is an act of trust and a form of contract. In many ways, your ass belongs to them after that. I'm not about having relationships based on ownership. She is her own person and I want to keep it that way.

Three days ago, I got a letter from my brother. Like an actual letter. Not an email, not a social media message, not a text. An honest to fuck letter. Hand written for fuck's sake. I have no idea how he got my post address. I don't typically use mail. Most folk in the world in which I inhabit have more direct or cryptically indirect ways of reaching a person than relying on the United States Postal Service. These days, little surprises me.

I haven't opened it. I'm not sure why I was delaying. I just felt like whatever was on the other side of that #10 barrier would force my hand in some kind of way. Even if it was just the illusion of control, I didn't want to give up that nugget. I haven't seen him in twenty or more years. I disappeared and no effort was made to find me. I have made a career of finding lost things, even when I was not in the investigation business, I have always been seeking hard truths. The people in my previous life that were supposed to care most about me never lifted a finger to find me when I vanished. That bit of information was all I needed to move forward with my walk.

Yet here I was, sitting in a bar in Old Town, looking at an

unopened envelope from my brother. The envelope was written in his hand. He was left handed and a scientist and both of those things shone through in his handwriting. It was impossibly small and precise. He was all rationality and practicality, two things that I could never get in line with. I was a constant nuisance to him growing up and I could only assume I was a barnacle that he was endeavoring to cut off. Although he was never a person that needed closure. He just set a course and kept on moving.

I don't drink any more, but I still find myself in places that flourish in strong spirits. I am most comfortable with the element of society that operates in less polite modes. It just takes so much energy to keep up the mask of polite society, the act of keeping company with outcasts and refugees has always been more comfortable. I have never fit in anywhere and they never expect you to.

"You gonna open that?" Mikey called to me from across the bar.

"Haven't decided yet." I replied.

"I think you have." Mikey quipped with a half smile. "Otherwise you would've already thrown it in the trash."

Mikey wasn't altogether wrong. I usually didn't allow myself the comfort of internal conflict . I was all gut and fire. Make a call, don't look back. Yet there I was, gazing deeply into the inky waters of my past.

I was done with it, by rights I should have been done with it. I laid the

envelope on the bar. "It's from a person I haven't had to deal with in a

very long time." I told the Mikey the Bartender.

"What's the worst that can happen?" Mikey asked offhandedly.

"I try not to ask that question any more." I replied. I pulled a

twenty from my wallet and laid it on the bar. "If she asks, I wasn't here."

I told him.

"If She asks, I'm gonna tell her what she wants to know because

I'm not a damn fool. I'll take your money, but I am not agreeing to

suicide." Mikey replied.

"Fair enough." I said.

I picked up the envelope and walked out of the bar. It was a long

walk home, I was largely trapped in my own head. The nightlife was as it

always was and always shall be, a static thing in this world of chaos. I

reached my apartment and found my resolve to open the letter.

I read it over, it was a simple no frills appeal to me to come home.

Back to the source of all that pain. Back to Michigan. More specifically back to Brighton. I did not care for Brighton. I didn't care for it then, and I am willing to bet that I don't care for it now.

About halfway down the page, my brother said something about some family business that needed to be tended to. And as I am family, I should be part of the process. Family. That's a word that never had much trade with me. I kept closer to Grandad than anyone, and mostly because he died when I was 19, so the relationship was much simpler. The dead are easy to get along with, it's the living that are a pain in the ass.

I knew I had to go right away. Not because it was him telling me to come out. Fuck him. I had to go because in addition to whatever bullshit needed tending to back in my hometown, I had dealings back home that needed my undivided attention. There was way too much that I had been running from for the past couple decades. Now that I wasn't the Sorcerer Supreme, I had the time and mental energies to deal with them. Funny how being responsible for the sins of the World makes a person lose focus on the petty nonsense that follows you around like a lost puppy. Ironically now that I had the time and mental energies, I lacked the limitless mystical powers to dispatch said problems.

Maybe this made it more worthwhile. You know, like a Greek legend of man overcoming his inherent flaws to prove his divinity. Or maybe this was my comeuppance for not dealing with shit in a timely manner. Maybe none of that was right and it was just my ego and my sense of guilt battling one another for a share of my attentional space. Maybe all three choices, who knows. All I knew is that I had to go, and sooner rather than later.

Esmarelda couldn't come with me. I didn't want to leave her behind, but I knew it was for the best. She is a lit stick of dynamite. She packs a mean punch, but if you're not ready for her to go off, sorry about your luck, friend. You knew what this was before you signed on, or at least you better had damn well knew what this was. Either way, if you carry it around it's your mess. I was always better at leaving things in the rearview than I was at nurturing them into anything worthwhile. I was not just attracted to the Death Energy by happenstance. I move the wheel. It's all I've ever really done well.

I packed up my shit in a backpack and headed for the door. The Chupacabra looked at me with and-where-the-fuck-do-you-think-you're-going cock to his head.

"Take care of her, will you?" I asked. He said nothing and ambled off to the bedroom to lie back down. I knew a guy who had a plane and owed me a favor. I made a call and he met me at his local airfield in the middle of the night. It was that kind of favor. The kind you can't question.

He was all gassed up and so was the plane. We made off for the East, flying over the embodiment of light pollution that was Las Vegas. Once we got out of the city, and out of King County, everything was a vast nothingness beneath us. We were riding high inside the void. I was left with his K-Pop and my thoughts.

Jeb was something of an oddity. I never asked him about his life choices, honestly it didn't have fuckall to do with me, but something always struck me odd about a smuggler cowboy that listened to K-pop. It was like some kind of a joke that I was never let in on the punchline to. You laugh reflexively out of courtesy, but you never really know why it was funny. A lot of my life has been like that over the years. I was smart enough to know how I should be acting but never having the social intuition to know why.

Jeb must have caught me staring. He piped over to me over the music.

"You alright there, buddy?" He asked.

"About as alright as I get." I replied.

"I need a bearing, Neil." Jeb said.

"Take me to Detroit." I answered. I closed my eyes and drifted off to sleep.

Chapter 2: Back to the Murder Mitten

I'd like to say that I got a lot of restful sleep and awoke fully renewed. That would have been a lie. We touched down at the airport in Detroit just after 4AM. Not that airport in Detroit. The one you're thinking of is actually in Romulus which is about 20 miles West of Detroit. The one I landed in is actually in city limits and is now named after one of the city's most corrupt politicians. No, not him. Not the one you're thinking of. The other guy.

Once I was safe to do so, I disembarked the plane. Jeb met me around on the tarmac. We both stood apart from each other, Jeb shifting uneasily. We stood wordlessly for a good portion of time. I could see that he wanted to say something, but needed a push to get him moving. I tilted my head to the side and squinted.

"You alright there, Boss?" I asked Jeb

Jeb nervously dug at himself to get the words out, "We good?"

"Any debt you may have had with me, real or imagined, is forgiven." I replied

Jeb threw both of his thick, meaty arms around me and squeezed. "I'm real happy to hear that, Neil."

"You've subtly conveyed that emotion." I mumbled directly into his shoulder. "Now I need you to let me go." I stated.

Regaining his composure, Jeb let me go and dusted himself off. "Well then, I'm gonna mosey on down to the flight club and see what kind of ruckus I can raise." Jeb tipped his hat to me and sauntered on down the runway. No sooner did I turn away from him did I feel a gnawing in the pit of me. I was back in a place that I have not been in years, and in a way unlike any I had known before. As the famous quote reads, you can't go home again. And yet here I am.

I walked past the runway to the barriers. Hopping them effortlessly, I made my way to six mile Road. I cleared the light of the airport to find a cab waiting on the street.

To those of you unfamiliar with Detroit, let me explain something to you. There is no cab culture in Detroit. This ain't New York or Chicago. I mean, sure you can call a cab. But cabs don't just sit around places waiting to pick up fares. Especially not in that part of town right before dawn. Ain't nothing happening at that time in that place that you would be comfortable telling your gramma about. As I approached the street, the cab flashed its lights. Never being accused of being particularly wise, I walked up to the cab.

Having been slightly obscured by mist, I didn't make out the cabbie from inside the car.

For fuck's sake

"Hey there Mr. Hawthorne." Luke called from inside the cab.

"Luke what the fuck are you doing in Detroit?" I asked

"Same thing I do everywhere, buddy. Drive cab. Hey, you go where the work is." He answered.

"Fair enough." I slung my backpack off and climbed in the passenger's seat. "Cool if I ride up front?" I asked.

"Absolutely, sir." Luke replied. "Where to?"

"Well, as this is a business trip, let's start with my long fucking list of business to tend to." I pulled out a scroll about the size of what you would imagine Santa Claus's list of good little children would look like. This was pretty far from that. This was more like the naughty list. "First stop should be Old Mariner's. I need to let the troops know I'm in town before they hear from someone else."

"Right-o" Luke replied. He popped the taxi into gear and we headed off for the church.

I laid my head back on the headrest. My chest was feeling heavy and tight. Not sure if that was the sign of an impending heart attack or impending alcohol relapse, but I was riding it out to see where I landed. I had a lot to do and no real timeline other than my own conscience in which to complete it. The mundane tasks were considerably more complex than the mystical ones, so naturally I would put them off to the end of my time here. If I get to them at all.

"That would be just like you." I heard a feminine voice from the backseat. I snapped alert and spun around to see who was with us. "Forget something?" She asked.

Fuck. It was Esmarelda. She was dressed in a leather jacket and had her hair pinned up in waves. Her makeup was flawlessly executed and I could read across her face that she was none too pleased with me at that moment.

"Oh hi, dear. I bet you want." I started to explain but she cut me off.

"I don't want shit." She replied curtly. "You did what you did.

Cool. But you don't get to make that call. I haven't put this work in to see you fuck it all away by doing some stupid shit like getting yourself killed." She took a drag off a djarum that I did not notice was lit. "Or worse."

"I'm sorry." I half-whispered, half-mumbled

"Fuck your sorry." She let slip an icy reply. "You're not sorry yet but you will be". She took another drag and said nothing more until we reached Old Mariner's Church.

We pulled up to the church. Luke drove around to an alley around back and parked. I got out. Luke jumped out and let Esmarelda out of the back seat. She thanked him with a peck on the cheek. Luke nervously re-entered his cab and drove away. I slung my pack over my shoulder.

We stood silently in the footprint of Old Mariner's Church. It was a rare moment when I didn't have words, but that was clearly one of them. I derived no pleasure from leaving her. I just lacked the skills that were required in negotiating how to tell about what I had to do and why.

"Ok" Esmarelda said. "I've cooled off a bit. I'm ready to hear your piss poor excuse." She chuckled, "I mean what you have to say for yourself."

I took in a breath and slowly let it out.

"I..." I started and was immediately cut off

"How the fuck are you just gonna leave like that?" She tore into me. "No note, no text, no call. I had to find out from the dog. The fucking dog, Neil! Is that how you do things?"

"Generally yes." I said quietly, "But..."

"Well it's shit. You need to do better." She took a puff. "You need to be better." She paused to regain herself. "I know I have a lot of baggage, but we're a team. You can't just leave me out of your struggles when you think I may get hurt by them, Neil."

"I was trying to keep you safe," I replied.

"I'm a big girl. I can decide my own risks." She paused and narrowed her eyes. "and whether they are worth taking. That shit should mean something to you, of all people."

I nodded. "It does. I didn't know what to do, so I ran away. It's an old defence and yeah, I need to do better. This trip is about going back to the beginning and fixing some of that bullshit" I said.

"Every ding in your armor is a story of how you came to be, Neil. Don't pitch the suit just because you think a shiny new one would be better. The you that learned to move in that damaged suit would never manage in a brand new one. Kindly remember that. And that damaged fucker is the one I'm quite fond of. I would appreciate it if you don't go murdering him with all your misguided self help bullshit." A smile peeked out the corner of her lip. As furious and terrifying as she can be, it passes just as quickly. Part of the joy of being with her is never knowing which you are getting. No skilled sailor is made in calm waters.

"This isn't all about self-improvement, Esmarelda. This is about taking care of some shit I should've put to rest last time I was here. I didn't have the strength then, and I probably don't have the power now. But I gotta take a chance to make this right." I said.

"You got one thing now that you didn't then." Esmeralda informed

"What's that?" I asked, looking at the looming facade of the church.

"You've got a me." She winked.

"That I do," I replied.

I took her hand and we walked up the steps, to the door of the Old Mariner's Church.

Chapter 3: Detroit, Rock City

Esmarelda still in tow, I raised my hand to knock on the door of Old Mariner's Church. A moment before my knuckle connected, the massive oaken door swung open slowly and gently. I turned to look at my traveling partner, her gaze fixed determinedly at the path ahead.

Without deviating her gaze, she uttered through clenched teeth, "Let's fucking do this."

Hand in hand, we crossed the threshold of the church.

The interior neve was lit with incandescent torchlight. A middle aged woman, slender and dignified was sitting at a table writing. She rose, her black robes draping the floor around her. She picked up the book she was writing in and walked toward Esmarelda and myself.

"That's close enough, sister." Esmarelda spoke sternly.

I chuckled.

"What's so fucking funny, Neil?" Esmarelda chided.

As the woman came closer, it became clear that she was wearing the vestments of a catholic nun.

"Sister, indeed." I said with a cocked smile.

"Hardy har." Esmeralda retorted.

"What seek you, friends?" The Sister asked.

"I've been away from town for a long time, but I am looking for some friends of mine. They used to use this Church as a base of operations, in a manner of speaking." I answered

The Sister moved within a few feet of us. With her so close, I was able to get a much better look at her. I laughed, this time a bellow. "Natasha! I didn't recognize you with all that shit on."

A broad, toothy smile flashed across her face, revealing two needle-sharp incisors "You've found me out."

Esmarelda spun around to me, moving all attention away from the newly discovered Natasha. Natasha removed her habit, a cascade of wavy red hair spilling down over her robes.

"Who the fuck is this bitch? She says to herself" Esmarelda spoke as if she were performing an aside.

"This, my friend, is Natasha. We used to, um, work together when I was with the Resistance." I said.

"She's a vampire, Neil. You knew that, right?" Esmarelda asked, black eyes burning like coal.

"I was aware, yes." I answered Esmeralda as if the object of our conversation were not standing feet away from us.

"Hmm. Okay then." Esmarelda walked away from me and started inspecting the altar.

"How have you been?" Natasha asked me.

"I've been." I answered. "You look exactly as the last time I saw you."

"No shit." Esmarelda barked from across the room. "That's part of the shtick."

"She's just lovely," Natasha said sarcastically. "Really, what brings you back to Detroit?" She asked.

"Business. Righting some old wrongs." I answered.

"The Sigils?" Natasha asked.

"That's part of it to be sure." I answered

"Not much of the old crew is left. It's just me, the Templar, and the Professor. The rest of them split town after we dealt with the Kosars." Natasha said. "There are some new ones though."

"More Delphi recruits?" I asked with trepidation

"They got really busy once they figured out how to replicate the formula." She said with her gaze turned down.

"I'm here to destroy sigils, not have a class reunion." I said.

"Understood." Natasha answered.

"But you did tell me what I needed to know. The old guard is turned over. This is going to be an interesting trip to be sure." I reached for Natasha's hand, put it to my lips and kissed the back of it. "You're still a marvel."

"Be careful, Neil. You're not so young any more." Natasha cautioned.

"Alright Ez, let's get." I suggested. Esmeralda wordlessly walked out the front door, with me following close behind. The door closed itself behind us as we left.

"So. About that." Esmarelda said.

"Yeah. She looks good." I said.

"Do you have like a punch card for supernatural beings that you're fucked, or what?" Esmarelda barbed. "Because like I think you're eligible for a toaster or something."

"Jealous?" I asked.

"If you want to stick your dick in an animated corpse, that's on you." Esmarelda laughed.

I joined her in the revelry.

Luke pulled up in the cab. The two of us got in.

Luke turned to me, "where to?" he asked.

"I laid a number of sigils in and around the city to seal it from a demonic invasion. I need to undo the seals." I answered.

"I have no idea what the fuck you are tlaking about, Mr. Hawthorne. But I will take you wherever you want." Luke said with a smile.

"Let's head over to Central Station" I answered.

"Right-o" Luke answered.

Esmarelda looked quietly out the window. I was worried. If my time with her has taught me anything, she is deadlier silent than she is making a fuss. I much prefer the rumble of the thunder over the cut of the lightning.

Chapter 4: Trains!

Central Station was a location of great historical significance to the city of Detroit. It meant more than any amount of bike lanes or overpriced coffee houses could ever amount to. It was once the hub of transit in and out of what was once regarded as the Paris of the West. Now all that exists within these grounds is the memory of what once was and the promise to kill that memory in the name of progress.

I waved a thank you to Luke and he drove off. I used to try to leave money on his seat as a payment, but I kept finding it back in my pocket later on. These days I don't even bother. It is equally wasteful of my effort and insulting to Luke's integrity.

Central Station is currently the object of a renovation project and the jewel in the crown of New Detroit. It was never about the train station. The purpose of Central Station is that there was a flow of energy that moved through it. Once upon a time, there were Builders and these Builders would make great structures upon Ley Lines, the flowing life's blood of the energies of Gaea, the Earth Mother, herself. That's not the way buildings are made today. It is truly a lost art, and anyone who remembers it is laughed off or run out of town on the very rails that are not used anymore.

The site of one of the sigils of containment that I placed was on the floor of Central Station. I know what you're thinking. If the building is getting a renovation and/or demolition anyway why does it matter? The sigil would get destroyed or painted over and would be rendered inert. See, that's where you would be wrong. If the sigil is destroyed without first being disenchanted it becomes part of the fabric of the place forever. Even if the building no longer stands. It becomes part of the air of a place. That is why at Central Station more than any of the other five sites I needed to disenchant. It was a mistake I made long ago and needed to fix before it was an unfixable permanency.

We got within a few hundred feet of the station when Esmarelda stopped moving forward.

"What?" I asked. "What are you doing?"

"This is a bad thing, Neil. You shouldn't be doing this." Esmarelda said.

"I have to do this. It is my mistake and I need to fix it." I replied.

"I think you're looking at this all wrong. Let me explain." She gathered herself. I could tell I was in for a real treat so I just settled in to listen to what I had in store. "You used these sigils to contain a demon or somesuch, right?"

"Affirmative" I replied

"Why is this demonic entity in need of liberation?" She asked.

"I wrongly confined him. He was the tear in the fabric that set into motion the events that led us to meet."

"Okay. Two things are wrong with that. One, you did what you needed to do at the time. Own that shit and move on. Two, if you hadn't done what you did we would not have met. Everything happens for a reason. Sometimes the reason is you make shitty decisions but ultimately the end result is something salvageable." She smirked.

"Are you implying that if I undo this, it will undo us?" I asked, dumbfounded.

"I'm not implying shit. I'm outright saying it. Esmarelda stood with her arms crossed. "You're so focused on making things right, you can make out the right that you have."

Then it hit me. A garbage truck.

Lying in a heap on the side of the street, the wind and piss knocked out of me, I heard the air brakes engage as the driver ran over to me. "Holy shit, are you okay?"

"No." I answered. "I'm hurt pretty bad. Is she ok?"

"She who? You were standing alone in the street." The driver answered. He was just a kid. Couldn't have been twenty years old. I looked up at him and he had an odd halo around him. Must have been the lights of the truck behind him. "I need to get you to a hospital."

"No. You. Do. NOT." I demanded.

"What are you talking about? I'm calling an ambulance." The kid reached into his pocket and grabbed a mobile. He started dialing. I could hear a faint beeping sound in the distance, like the kind of thing you imagine hearing in a hospital or the beginning of a new wave synthpop song.

Beep. Beep. Beep. Beep.

It was so rhythmic. It had to be part of a vast hallucination from when I was hit. I knew I wasn't in a hospital though. I could feel every fiber of my broken body on fire. If I was in a coma, I would be sedated. And where was Esmarelda?

Beep. Beep. Beep. Beep.

There it was again. Shit. The kid was dialing.

"Yeah, there's been a car wreck. My location? I'm by Central Station. No, I'm not messing...hello. Hello? Are you there?" The kid trailed off. "They fucking hung up." He muttered to himself. "I can't let you just die"

Beep. Beep. Beep. Be Boop.

The fuck?

Beep. Beep. Beep. Be Boop.

Okay now I knew I wasn't in some hospital bed working through a coma. That was definitely new wave synthpop. I looked up at the sobbing man-child aheap above me. The beeping was getting louder and more rhythmically defined. Now I could smell a hint of rosewater in the wind.

Oh for fucks sake.

A shadow moved past the halo issuing from behind the garbage truck driver from his right across to his left. I could only move my eyes at this point, but I looked over toward where I had thought the shadow had gone.

"You son of a bitch." I said, spitting up blood.

"I'm sorry, mister. I'm sorry." The driver devolved again into a sniveling fit.

"You need to get the fuck out of here kid. I mean now." I coughed the last bit of my energy out as I gurgled up blood.

I could now clearly make out the robed figure of the Grim Reaper. The beep was coming from him. In his arms was not his characteristic scythe, but a vintage Roland Ax-Synth in Black with Silver Trim.

Motherfucker must have had it made custom. That shit only came in red. He came to party.

"I have been waiting so long for you, Neil Hawthorn." The reaper hummed.

"That's great." I hacked. "What's with the Keytar?"

"I'm trying out a thing." The Grim Reaper replied. "Is it working for me?"

"It has an aesthetic, but I'm not sure it's what you want." I replied.

"Mileage may vary, I guess" The Grim Reaper replied. "It's time Neil."

"I need a mulligan!" I spit out in a rush.

"A what now?" The Grim Reaper asked.

"A mulligan. Like in Golf, a do-over" I gasped.

"And on what grounds do you think..." The Grim reaper chided.

Mid Sentence a burst of Blue-Green Light burst out from my chest, enveloping the Grim Reaper in incandescence. The Reaper covered his face and backed away from my broken body. The light became more and more obtrusive until he was forced back through into the Underworld.

"...and in strange aeons even Death may die" I said to myself as I drifted away into unconsciousness.

I woke up with my head resting on Esmarelda's shoulder.

"What the fuck was that back there?" She asked me.

'What back where?" I asked, still a bit hazy.

"That blast of light with the Reaper." She prompted.

"Turning in my punch card." I chuckled. "Where are we?" I asked.

"On a ghost train heading to Ann Arbor" Esmarelda replied. "Shhh. Just let it happen."

As for how I was still alive and largely unscathed, I tried not to think about that either.

Chapter 5: Tree City, USA

The train pulled into the Amtrak station amidst a cloud of smoke. We deboarded the spectral locomotive and it promptly dissolved into a tangible fog. No better way to travel. If you find yourself with the opportunity to ride on a ghost train, I highly recommend it. Surprisingly comfortable for not actually having any component that is made of corporeal matter.

"Neil, I want to tell you something that I did not mention before. I am actually from Ann Arbor." Esmarelda said.

"Bullshit." I replied.

Her face was slack jawed. "What?" she barked.

"You heard me. That is utter bullshit. You're not from anywhere. You're from fucking Arcadia." I walked down Depot street toward Main.

"This is the town of the Lost. I have a history here. The City of Trees has a strong resonance with my kind. You need to know that before we get any further." Esmarelda grabbed both of my hands. "Do you understand?" She spoke while staring into my eyes. Her eyes cut right through my defences.

"Look, doll. I know you've been around the block. I don't care about any of that. I have a job to do and you said you'd help me." I stated.

"When did I say I was helping you?" Esmarelda laughed. "But I do have someone you need to meet."

"I can't wait. Is he like you?" I asked.

"He's something." She replied. "Let's go to Necto"

Necto was a nightclub. Mainly known for being the most gay-friendly establishment in a 20 mile radius. Back when I was a kid it used to be called the Nectarine Ballroom and was exclusively a gay danceclub. I guess nowadays it goes by Necto as a rebranding effort to make it more hip. As if they needed any help looking cool, everything in this town was painfully trendy in a self-effacing kind of way. It was almost as if everything in Ann Arbor was trying as little as possible to appear as if it were trying too hard.

I fucking loathe this town but can't help but love it. We picked up some electric scooters and zipped across town to Necto. There was a line out to Liberty St. The bouncer spotted Esmarelda and waved us up to the front of the line.

"Hey Aisling, what's good?" The Bouncer asked

"Oh hey Diesel. Every day is exactly the same." Esmarelda replied flatly

"Girl, I know that's right." He replied. "Who's the straight?" He asked

"Oh honey. He's no straight." She replied. Feigning a whisper, she placed a hand on the side of her mouth "He plays with the Dead." She said to Diesel.

"Man, you're a freaky one, huh?" Diesel asked me.

"Sure." I said in a disinterested tone. "I don't really want to be here."

He didn't seem to hear me . "Come on in." Diesel told us "Don't make us wait so long next time, lady." He said to Esmarelda.

"Yeah, no promises." Esmarelda said with a smirk.

We got our hands stamped and made our way into the club. Everything was obnoxiously dark except for the random glow sticks placed around for ambiance. Trying to look like they cared enough to give things an atmosphere but not so much that they wanted actual functioning lights.

As we entered the darkened antechamber every part of us reverberated with goth dance beats, even down to our fetid souls.

We crossed the stairway scaffolding up to the mezzanine and to the dance floor. There were not too many club denizens on Industrial night. Probably about thirty or forty regulars and a handful of first timers. The dance floor was not exceptionally crowded, but there was a clustering of

dancers around the perimeter of the floor. Off in the corner was a man

that could only be described as humping the radiator.

Scanning away, there was a clubgoer dancing alone in the center of

the floor. He possessed the attention of everyone who gazed upon him. In

his presence, one could not help but stare. He owned the dancefloor, the

bar room, the mezzanine and everything in between. His every movement

was an incantation and he was dripping with venom awaiting his next

victim of dance based hypnosis.

Esmarelda leaned in close to me. "There he is. Mister

Winthrope." She spoke.

Winthrope spotted Esmarelda and broke his spell. He ran over to

her and lifted her off the ground with an embrace. "Marcy, are you really

here?" He asked.

"As here as one can be and as real as I ever am" She answered.

"Fair enough." He replied.

He looked at me with a sudden startle, as if I had been there when

he walked over and just appeared. "Can I help you, sir?" His voice was

dripping with sarcasm.

"I doubt it." I replied.

"Well, well. You are equipped with a rather poor attitude. You have no way of knowing what I can or cannot do for...or to you." He narrowed his eyes at me.

"What is this?" I asked bluntly. "Are we supposed to have some fucking danceoff or something? You gonna prove that I'm not good enough to be here? News flash, I'm not. So save your scissors, Cutman. I'm not the one for you." I walked away and made myself a seat at the bar.

Winthrope turned to Esmarelda. "He's a miserable piece of shit, huh?"

Esmarelda replied, "Yeah. He kind of is. It's part of his charm." She chuckled.

"I fail to see the benefit in that." Winthrope replied.

"He needs your help, Francis." Esmarelda cut to the quick. "He just doesn't know it yet."

"He's going to have to ask me for it." Winthrope said with a glint in his eye.

"I know." Esmarelda assented. "Just go easy on him"

"You say that as if I know how." Winthrope quipped.

I sat at the bar. I watched as patrons moved back and forth through the line of getting and paying for drinks while I sat there static. The bartender leaned over to me, her multi colored braids dangling between us. "Look handsome, I'm gonna need you to buy something if you're gonna sit here"

I pondered whether I should. A nice gin with a wedge of lime sounded like the perfect solution to this situation. With my non-response, her polite flirtation turned to irritation. I opened my mouth to speak and felt a tug at my sleeve.

"We're getting out of here" I heard Esmarelda speak into my ear.

"Well. Guess that makes my decision for me", I said to the bartender. She turned away with a huff. I stood from the stool and turned around to see Esmarelda and Winthrope. Standing at the ready.

"What's this about?" I asked.

"We're going to go somewhere quieter and have a chat" Esmarelda said. Winthrope. Stood with a shit eating grin.

"Sure" I assented.

The motley crew of us left the club together and walked down the street to a cafe. It was a local place trying not too hard to avoid it's similarities to the burnt coffee Mecca of Seattle. Esmarelda got us coffees while Winthorpe and I found a spot to set up shop.

We looked at each other uncomfortably. I couldn't figure out what his game was. He was painfully optimistic about whatever was in his mind, but he wasn't about to share that nugget of information with me. He reached into his coat and pulled out a wooden case. An impossibly large wooden case from where he produced it.

"How?" I uttered.

"The question you should be asking is what?" Winthrope corrected me.

"Okay smartass. What?" I complied.

"Much better". He smiled and opened the case. He produced a checkerboard and laid it out on the table. "We are going to play some chess"

"I don't play chess," I replied.

"You haven't played chess, not yet," Winthorpe corrected. "we are going to play chess now". Winthrope started setting up the board in the initial piece formation.

"Do you know the rules?" He asked.

"I know the rules" I scoffed. "Everyone knows the rules"

"You'd do best to forget them. Remember how the pieces move but everything else is garbage"

I sat puzzled. He finished setting up the pieces and motioned to me.

"You have the first move" he prompted.

I moved my right center pawn forward two spaces. The same move I've done every game of chess I have played in my life.

"Your move" I said.

"It has become apparent that you do not know how to play chess. I will teach you though" Winthrope said with an excited smile that made me ache inside.

"I told you I don't play chess". I said through clenched teeth.

"Chess isn't about chess. The pieces don't matter. The moves don't matter. Chess is about problem solving. Just spending an hour or less with you has told me everything I need to know." Winthrope moved his opposite pawn to block mine. "you bash your fists into walls until they break. Somewhere along the line you were given powers to make your fists harder but your skills did not improve. Now you have weaker punches but are acting like you still have Iron gauntlets". He paused. "Your move"

I moved another pawn forward two spots.

"Okay." He said. "we're done here". He started packing up the pieces.

"What the Hell?" I shouted, attracting the attention of the other customers. "This is bullshit"

Winthrope slammed the case down. He jammed a finger into my chest. "No! What's bullshit is your lack of respect. This, like all things, is a dance. You aren't even looking at me. Just trying to figure out how to fuck me."

Esmeralda walked up with three coffees in to go cups. "Ope. I guess that's that."

Breaking the standoff, I turned to Esmarelda. "Did you just say ope?"

"Shit. I did". The three of us laughed.

The lesson in that moment I learned didn't come from the proposed teacher and wasn't even about chess. It was not to take shit too seriously. And sometimes you need an outside force to remind you of that.

Esmarelda and I parted ways with Winthrope. She gave him a warm embrace and he clumsily reciprocated. We walked a block to State St to see Merideth parked on the corner quite illegally. We hopped in and sped away.

"Thank you," Esmarelda said to me, looking out the window of the Cadillac.

"For what?" I asked.

"For indulging my whims" she said then fell quiet.

I didn't say anything more. That moment was too pure and innocent to fuck up with one of my tone deaf nihilism jokes. Sometimes you just have to let a sentiment breathe and fill the void. I've found there are small ways to fill that void, but they are fleeting and delicate. She reached over and placed her lace gloved hand on my thigh. This was probably all the redemption I deserved and more than I could have hoped for.

Esmarelda learned her head on my lap as I drove. She wasn't asleep and she wasn't fondling me either. I could tell that her energy levels were fading, but I also didn't feel it was right to take advantage of a self-driving car to get road head. I mean, is it even road head if there is no risk involved? Isn't it just head at that point?

"Oh!" I felt her voice vibrate excitedly through my trousers.

"Hmm?" I answered in an attempt to appear that I wasn't acutely aware of her face inches away from my clothed member.

"I need to pick something up." She said.

"Well you've already done that." I said luridly.

"Not that, stud. AT least not right now." She replied. "I need a book"

"So, you want to hit a bookstore or something?" I asked.

"A very specific bookstore. It's in Ypsi on Cross Street." She said

"Meredith?" I asked the Cadillac. "Is that enough info for you to get us there?" I felt the wheel altering course in accordance with the plan. "Okay then. there that's a thing we know." I mused to Esmarelda.

"Now about that other thing." She said with a smile and started to unzip my fly.

"If you insist" I agreed, allowing her to get a recharge.

We arrived at the bookstore a few minutes after I arrived.

The place was dark and the windows were cracked from years of neglect and attempts at vandalism.

"You sure this is the place?" I asked Ez.

"Oh yeah, this is the place." She confirmed.

We exited the vehicle and walked up to the bookstore. The store did not only appear to be permanently closed, but the frontage was completely unlabelled. The only way it was apparent to even be a bookstore was the horde of books piled up in every corner of the establishment that was visible from the storefront.

"I think this place is abandoned, Ez." I said. "Let's go to Barnes…"

Esmarelda put a hand on my mouth and stopped me from speaking. "Don't you dare say that name." She went no further to explain why. "We are going here and that is just that."

"Suit yourself." I said with a shrug.

Esmarelda walked to the door. She fussed with the doorknob. "Must be stuck" Another few seconds of struggling and the door sprung open. "There we go." She entered the darkened book lair. After a momentary hesitation, I followed in after her.

The bookstore was the exemplar of a fire hazard. Books were stacked floor to ceiling and the air was thick with must. I coughed loudly.

"Shh." Esmeralda quieted me. "You need to respect this place."

I heard the hum of a fluorescent bulb lighting up. Then in succession, the rest illuminated. I look up at the bank of hanging lights nervously. I swear there were papers leaning against them jammed into the rafters. I had a bad feeling about this. I heard sounds coming from the back room. I prepared myself for a coming conflict.

"Hello?" I heard a male voice come from the back.

"Hi!" Esmarelda called in a gentle, mousy voice unlike any I have heard her use.

The shop owner emerged from the threshold of the back room. "Theresa!" He called out joyously. He crossed to Esmarelda and gingerly gave her a hug. I didn't question why he was calling her Theresa. After all, Esmarelda wasn't her real name either. I didn't really want to know her real name. "What brings you in tonight?" He asked.

"This is my friend, Neil. He is in town to take care of some old baggage." Esmarelda explained. "I wanted to drop by and get a book from you and as well introduce the two of you."

"Well, first thing's first. What book do you need?" The book keeper inquired.

"The Philosophy of Time Travel by Roberta Sparrow." Esmarelda answered.

The Book Keeper gave "Theresa" a sly smile. "I think I have a copy of that around." He turned to leave. "How rude of me." He turned back in an awkward about face. "Where are my manners?" The book keeper walked to me with an outstretched hand, as if it was being externally yanked from his body "My name is Xander."

I took Xander's hand to shake it. I felt an odd familiarity about him, but couldn't quite identify why. He maintained direct eye contact with me and had a permagrin on his face. "Do I know you?" I asked. His smile widened.

"I'm familiar with your work, Mr. Hawthorne". Xander gave me an awkward wink. "I want to thank you for taking care of that little problem a ways back."

As if I weren't nervous enough, I became doubly so. "Which problem would that be?" I asked.

"The Doro problem." Xander snickered.

"Look, I didn't kill." I started to defend myself.

Xander held his hands up, interrupting my speech. "Say no more. On behalf of my colleagues, I just wanted to say thank you. We don't have to work quite so hard to clean up his messes any more."

I was less confused as I was concerned. Xander left to retrieve the book from the hold in the back.

I turned to Esmarelda. "So, Theresa, why so interested in Time Travel all of a sudden." I asked.

"There's a lot about me you don't know." Esmarelda replied.

"Fair enough." I replied. "I'm gonna go outside and have a smoke across the street. You know, so not as to light the block on fire." I walked out the door and lit up a cigarette just outside the store. Esmarelda came out two sticks later with a book in her hand. "That it?" I asked.

"Yep. Let's get out of here." She went over to the Caddy and hopped in. I followed after.

Next stop, Brighton.

Chapter 6: The House of Long Shadows

We pulled up to the house on Fairlane. It was a brown and brick ranch located on what was once farmland. It still lies on a dirt road faithful to it's agrarian upbringings but there are many more homes on the street than when I was a child. It was an isolating place but one in which I never felt alone.

A massive crimson maple stood between the house and a small rental home that was also owned previously by my parents and inhabited by my Grandmother. Both are now vacant. The only constant in life is change. The wheel turns whether we turn it or not.

"You have got to be fucking kidding me!" Esmarelda exclaimed. "You spent your childhood in that?!?"

"I wouldn't call it much of a childhood but yes, I grew up there"

"That house is full of ghosts" Esmeralda told me

"It sure is, Ez. It sure is" I replied

I cut the ignition and exited Merideth. I shut the door and it sounded like the slamming of a great vault. The clang echoed in my mind. I walked over to the passenger side.

"You getting out?" I spoke to esmarelda through the rolled up window.

"Nah. I'm good. You do you." She replied.

"Are you afraid of ghosts?" I taunted

"It's not the ghosts I'm worried about. It's that fucking thing." She motioned at an empty space in the fenced in backyard. Clearly she saw something I did not. Some mixture of a loss of my supernatural sight and my desensitized survival strategy to being in that place for so long. Something dwelled back there and would be dealt with in time. But not until I had my business handled.

I entered my ancestral home through the open garage door, holding grandad's watch in my pocket against my palm. Everything was cold, even for November. My breath was visible in the air as I exhaled. Everything was more or less as I remembered it. The wood panelling on the living room walls. The velvet Matador painting on the wall behind the couch. There was something inviting about the static nature of the place.

I knew my parents were gone, but it was as if I could still hear them there. To be clear, this was not the spirits of my parents, this was my memory of the life I had with them before I disappeared. I pulled open the drawer in the kitchen that always stuck a little. Gave it a jiggle to get the rest of the way open. The junk drawer, an accumulation of a lifetime of random ass shit, was as screw-ball as it ever had been. I menagerie of electrical tape rolls, test lights, corroded batteries (what the fuck were you saving these for, Dad?) and loose nails and screws. In the bottom of the drawer was a key.

"Disco." I muttered to myself quietly.

A light flickered in the hallway. Fuck. I quickly threw the ancient skeleton key in my pocket and looked down the hall. The light did not appear to be electrical. It had to be some kind of candle. I took a few steps toward it and stopped. I looked down at my feet. I stopped at the edge of where the kitchen tile met the carpet in the dining room. I could not bring myself to cross it. That dining room was where we had our family dinners and played cards when visitors came by. Even having less than stellar recollection of the time I spent in Hawthorne Manor, it was my point of origin and still had considerable gravity.

I drew a deep breath and crossed the tackboard threshold.

As I grew closer to the hallway and the flicker of what I presumed to be candlelight, I felt the house betting colder still. My breath was now

pillars of fog as I moved along. I got to the mouth of the hall and stopped

again.

"Hey. It's Neil." I called down the hall.

The flickering stopped in response to my voice and became a

steady glow. I heard behind me the door to the basement swing open. Do

not fucking go in that basement, Neil.

Of course I walked back through the kitchen to the stairway. I

looked down the dark stair with concern. I should not go down there. Not

alone. Not ever, really. I found myself reflexing stepping onto the stairs.

Neil, slow the fuck down. I made the thirteen steps by muscle memory

and stopped at the landing. It was black as pitch down there. I snapped

my fingers and produced a tiny light orb. A parlor trick really in the grand

scheme of magick, but a trick I still had nonetheless.

As the light spilled into the basement, I could see shadows

scurrying away around the corner to the refuge of the area behind the brick

and cedar bar that went unused throughout my childhood and was used

now for storage. I knew right away these were not animals.

The air was thick with mold. It was clear to me that my father had

not been able to keep up with maintenance in his failing health and the elements had gotten the better of the house. I placed a handkerchief over my mouth in an effort to not breathe any of the pre-asbestos code particulate matter into my lungs. I took a step off the landing onto the concrete floor, while my fairy orb floated alongside me. Disregarding the shadows milling about in the periphery, I made a hard left to the utility room. I placed a hand on the doorknob and turned it. It gave way with a nudge, expelling even moldier, staler air. Luckily I already had the cloth to my mouth or else would have been in a full blown asthma fit.

Every portion of the room was covered in a layer of spider-web and dust. I gingerly made my way to a handmade shelving unit that housed the last of the jars of canning that my mother had completed before the illness took hold. At least it is how I piece this together as a post-mortem based on what Terry had told me. The ideas I had drawn from our meeting were filling in gaps and functioning as memory and fact. I reached my arm to the back of the shelf, in an impossibly shaded spot, and felt around. I found a wooden chest, about the size of a shoebox. Just what I was looking for.

I picked up the box and heard a tiny, quiet voice come from the doorway.

"That does not belong to you." The voice spoke.

I froze. Not turning around, I answered. "I left this here years ago and you know damn well that I did." I swallowed hard, trying not to choke on the dust in my throat. "Now leave me be."

"You left the house to us, child." The voice said. "Put the box back"

"You can fuck right off" I replied with conviction.

"You should not have come here" The voice spoke again.

"Can't say I disagree, but I have business. You're just gonna have to be okay with that." I pulled the key from my pocket and placed it in the keyhole of the chest. I spun around to face the speaker. A shadow stood in the doorway. Despite the light being cast directly at the form, the shadow did not dissipate.

"It's been a very long time." The shadow spoke.

Ever since I was a child, before I even had cogent recollection of my memories, I have had experiences with ghosts of some stripe or other. The basement was always a focal point of that spiritual activity. When I turned 14, on my birthday, I decided to move from my bedroom upstairs to the basement. Why would I relocate myself to a place where I know spooks and spectres to reside? Because fuck them, that's why.

One night after about a month of living down there, I was having terrible, feverish nightmares. I awoke with a start. I could feel the air

leaving my body and my chest tightening. In the darkness of the

basement, as my eyes were adjusting to the available light, I saw the

remains of a shadowy figure reaching for me and slowly fading out of

existence. When the room returned to normal, I could breathe again and

was no longer feeling like I was not long for this world. I felt like this was

the same shadow. Just a hunch.

Face to face with it once again, despite my decade plus of being

the big dog wizard of Earth and years of mystical training, I felt very

much like a powerless tenneager again. I couldn't catch my breath. It was

if I had been struck in the chest with a baseball bat.

"You are nothing here, Necromancer." The shadow spoke. "You

should not have returned."

I gathered the strength I had remaining and opened the now

unlocked chest. There was a single object in it, a shiny buffalo nickel. I

had shined it with salt water when I was 6 and put it in that box and

promptly forgot about it, in case of a rainy day. I was obsessed with coins

back then. That never really changed. It was raining pretty hard right

now.

I flipped the coin in the air. The shadow floated backward out of the threshold.

"Oh, you don't care for this do you?" I taunted. I strode forward with the coin held aloft. The shadow retreated away from me as I walked forward. I headed directly to the landing and started walking backward up the stairs.

"You'll never escape my grasp, young one." The shadow spoke. "You can leave this place, but this place will never leave you."

"Fuck your grasp." I said as I got to the top of the stairs.

I exited the starway and immediately left the house.

As I got to the garage again, I saw the night sky outside lit as if the noonday sun was filling the sky.

When I stepped into the light, the Cadillac was already running and Esmarelda was laying on the horn.

"Get in the fucking car!" She yelled from the driver's side window.

I looked to the sky. A mass of swirling lights was moving in a cyclonic vortex in the sky over my parents house. I pointed at the rotating mass of luminosity and yelled to Esmarelda. "What the hell is that?!?"

The car lurched forward a few feet to close the gap between

it and myself. Unfortunately that also put them that much closer to the light tornado. The passenger door swung open.

"I'll explain when we aren't sucked into a supernatural phenomenon. Get your ass in the car" she commanded. I complied.

Esmarelda cut a switch back turn and sped off across the yard onto the rental house driveway. Gravel spit out behind us as we spun around the corner to get back onto fairlane. Everything was still Illuminated even a mile down the road.

"It doesn't seem to be following us" I said under my breath

"Not yet" Esmarelda replied. "but I don't intend to stick around and find out we are wrong."

The Cadillac continued hauling ass down the dirt road. We jacked the turn onto Field Crest toward 9 mile.

"Turn left here" I instructed. Esmarelda did as I asked. I directed them to a stand of trees off of 9 mile on the south side of the road. Something that would be a pull off for fishers. We pulled off the road and parked.

I got out of the car. The glow was still visible over the tree line looking northward. I peeked my head back in the car. "I know a guy here. I'm gonna ask some questions about what's going on. "

"Knock yourself out, lover. I see shit go down, I'm abandoning your ass." Esmarelda said with a wink.

About 30 years back, when I was still in elementary school, a kid named Jimmy was a school mate of mine. He went missing and the whole world turned upside down. It was the first time anyone had used the words child abduction. Well, long story short Jimmy was found a week later in that stand of trees. His body was just discarded and left for carrion critters. I focused myself. Like I said before, I don't have all of my powers, but I have some tricks. I reached into the fabric and pulled back the veil.

"Hey Jimmy." I whispered.

I heard a ten year old boy's voice answer me "Hey"

I opened my eyes. His gossamer silhouette stood in front of me. I found myself starting to tear up in the corners of my eyes. It was like the last time I saw him at school.

"Hey buddy. It's Neil". I spoke softly.

"I remember. You sat a few seats back from me and peed your pants in class" Jimmy said. I don't think Jimmy was being intentionally cruel. I didn't get that feeling from his words. Dying at ten has to do a number on a person's social development. I didn't expect him to have a ton of empathy with the living after how he went out. "You still into that dragon game?"

"Yeah, you got the right guy. I don't play many games these days" I answered. "being a grown-up stinks".

"I guess." He kicked the ground around his feet. "I won't know"

His words stopped my breath. I gathered myself. "I need your help, Jimmy. I know you know things. I have a question"

"Sure," Jimmy said innocently. "But I need a favor in return"

"Name your price." I said.

"I need you to deliver a message for me," Jimmy said. "I've tried to tell her myself, but she can't hear me"

"Ok. " I said with growing concern.

"Tell my mom I'm not mad at her. I know she blames herself for what happened. I want her to not be sad any more." Jimmy said with his eyes down.

"I will deliver the message. I promise". I said.

There was a long pause. "Okay Neil. What do you need to

know?" Jimmy asked.

"There is some weird stuff going on around my old house. You know the one I grew up in down the way. Weird stuff like I haven't seen before. What is it?" I asked.

Jimmy paused again a minute. "You know how sometimes you walk in a room, like after your parents had a fight that you weren't supposed to know about, and you can just feel it?"

"I do" I answered.

"That place is a place we don't go. We just know not to". Jimmy stopped. "It's a very bad place"

"Do you know why?" I asked.

"In a time long before our world, there was another world. Mankind came over from the other world and made this world their home. They came over a bridge at first and then the bridge broke. A big part of that bridge is in the ground. You grew up on it". Jimmy said.

"Oh..." I said with surprise

"That's all I know. Sorry Neil. Say hi to my Mom for me. Jimmy faded back into the wood.

I walked back to the car.

"I heard what the kid said. Damn my fairy ears." Esmarelda chuckled. "So looks like your demons weren't demons after all?"

"Moon Ghosts." I uttered.

"Damn moon Ghosts" Esmarlda replied.

"Precisely" I confirmed.

Chapter 7: Basic Cosmology

Now that we've gotten this far, I'm going to give you some basic background on the nature of the universe. My life as the Sorcerer Supreme was about keeping the mystic plane of Earth free from invasion by extra dimensional forces. That all sounds well and good but if you spend too much time on the metaphysical side of the equation it is very possible and highly likely that you will neglect the nature of physical reality. That's what this lesson is about.

We exist on a planet called Earth, Terra, Midgard. It has a number of names but the basic gist is the same. We have a home and it has us. We are a creature that we call human. Science has figured out what we are and how we developed for the most part. It's only mostly right. The governments of the world have been keeping a secret from you that acts as a fundamental flaw in the structure of the major religions of the world. Surprise motherfuckers, ain't nobody gonna let that information slip.

We come from Mars.

You read that right. Humanity, as a species, originates on

the red planet. It's not that simple either. We didn't just come over here on spaceships and set up shop.

Everything that biologists have figured out about genetic ancestry and evolution is accurate. But how we went from being single celled organisms to organizing into more complex critters is not entirely accurate. We didn't just do it randomly. There have been various nudges throughout the course of human history. Whenever this information has been shared with humanity it had to be done in really creative and fun ways so that the fragile human mind wouldn't warp in upon itself.

Enter: Religion. We heard a message. We passed that message from person to person and anyone who's played telephone knows how that goes. A prophet gets a piece of the puzzle and incompletely fills in gaps with non-factual information. Then of course politics gets involved. Yeah. So by the time it does get written down it is as if it was entirely created by the writer. Which in a way it was.

There are folks who have heard the word of the Creators and it drove them mad. There are others who were told they were mad. And still more that were killed to silence their knowledge. The truth is often a poison. In small doses it can cure ailments. But largely it just makes life unliveable. The advantage of being interdimensional or multiplanar is that the multiplicity of rules makes things more fast and loose. Truth becomes a figure of speech more than an actual structure.

Humanity was given a seed of infinite power by the Creators. This seed stays buried within the genetic code still today. As time has progressed these powers have emerged as the greatest figures in mythology. These so-called myths were dismissed by later cultures to control the message. But believe this, all of it is true.

There are sects of learning that have been gifted with the technological sciences of Mars. They were taught how to build towers, bridges, and pyramids. And they all serve specific purposes.

Where do Moon Ghosts come in, you may ask. Moon Ghost is an expression that the Arcadians, the fae, came up with because they were the first ones who encountered them in their home, the Moon. Yes fae come from the moon. Anyway. Yes there are real ghosts. Human energy patterns contained within their life energies have an impression that follows over into the plan of Death. Otherwise, I wouldn't have much of a job as a necromancer. But anywho...

When things go very fast, they break the time continuum. Like faster than light fast. Some creatures move opposite the directionality of time. The fae have termed them moon Ghosts to differentiate them from actual ghosts. They are essentially the energy impression of creatures that move so fast that they can cast a shadow back in time. And control it. So that is a moon ghost.

One of the gifts that Mars gave humanity was an entity known as the Dark Star. It is essentially a corporeal ball of evil. It was expelled from Mars as a byproduct of them perfecting themselves into godhood. The jettisoned ball of dankness ran smack into an uninhabited planet called Earth. Uninhabited except for the mythic creatures that existed before man. They waged war against this great evil. Some made great sacrifices. Others fled. All were affected.

That is why the Martians sent the seed of power. They felt guilty for cursing our planet with that damn Dark Star so they equipped mankind with hidden abilities they could develop and become demigods in their own right.

Scientists in the 1920's in a little thing called the Delphi Project figured out how to turn those switches on. You know like the apollonian Oracle? So they could Essentially make a demigod out of anyone. This project made a number of superhumans, many of whom still roam the streets. Some handled it. Some didn't. With great power comes something something.

The most notable of the experiment was the Topeka Five. In 1935 in Topeka, Kansas, five experimental subjects were made into metahumans. They went on to be a multinational peacekeeping force in World War II. The tricky part is that there was no peacekeeping so much as a covert team of assassins sent to take down the Nazi threat in Europe. After it was known that the German High Command was experimenting with metahumans of its own, Project Delphi decided to focus their efforts on closing up shop on Der Fuhrer and his buddies.

The five chosen went on to become Captain Justice, Kid Midnight, Mantis, Tabernacle, and the Countess. They spent the years from 1935 to 1943 dealing with supernatural threats that the Nazis were cooking up in Europe and abroad. The team disbanded after the war due to creative differences but Project Delphi

sponsored several superhuman groups designed to aid in the

continued existence of humanity against several wordly and

extraterrestrial threats.

That gets you caught up, I think. If there's more, I'll stop

again and add it. Being a wizard for so long fucked with my head,

but you know that already.

Chapter 8: The Sick and Dirty Truth

I signalled for Esmarelda to pull a u-turn and get on 23 going north. I looked at my window as we passed Fairlane along 23 and the lightshow had stopped. This did not provide me much solace though. I figured I would be able to get the nickle back and that would take care of my problems. Unfortunately it wasn't the answer to my Ills.

I guided my driver downtown to Grand River where we exited the freeway.

"So what happened in this place, Neil?" Esmarelda asked as she turned left onto Grand River.

"How far back do you want me to go?" I asked with a chuckle.

"As far as you need to, I guess." She replied.

"Well." I paused pensively. "Brighton was a town that got its start as a coach stop, but it goes back before that I reckon."

"Maybe I should have been more specific" Esmarelda was growing irritated. "When did this place get so corrupt?"

"I always knew this was a foul place but never could figure out why. People were always shit to each other and I couldn't wait to get the fuck out. A guy I knew, in fact a guy we both know, was a victim of major demonic possession here in this town when I was a teenager."

"Dorian?" Es asked

"Give that woman a gold star." I said sarcastically

"Eat shit and die, Hawthorn" She said with a glimmer in her eye.
"So, where to?"

"I think I know where we need to go. Keep driving, I'll tell you
when to turn." I instructed her. "Just watch out for cops. If they're
anything like when I was a kid, they're still assholes."

"Trust me, cops are the least of our worries." Esmarelda spoke
with determination.

We continued down Grand River toward Spencer, turning left on
Spencer. I had her turn left onto Leith St. We pulled up to 510 Leith and I
signalled to stop.

"Surprise, Surprise, Surprise." I said. "It's abandoned." I turned
to Esmarelda. "Hey, guess what."

"I don't know. It's haunted?" She scoffed.

"Exactly!" I smiled. "How did you know?"

"I swear I'm gonna smack the shit out of you, Neil. But you are
excellent company." She shook her head and rolled her eyes.

"This house here. This is the place it all went down. This is the house where Dorian Faust lived. He had a real shit life and almost had a real shitty death. Fortunately the gang of assholes that were trying to kill him fucked it all up and Dorian lived to play goth music another day."

"Who all was in on it? Anyone I know?" Esmarelda asked.

"That piece of shit, Doro, for starters. And a few other assorted unsavory types. A couple of Detroit's finest heroes, if you want to call them that. They heard that Dori was a vessel and came to purge him. Had they been successful, he would have been folded from this plane of existence. They couldn't get their shit together back in '94 so he ended up beat to shit and eventually the demon fled to another host. But he ended up making most of a recovery. Well, you know him. He was never quite right after that. To be honest, he was never quite right before that."

"He's a good fella." Esmarelda commented, "But he definitely is a different kind of cat."

"But before that even, when I was 8 or 9, I summoned a demon in my parents' old place. That's the reason why we're here. Not because my asshole brother asked me to. Not because I have some driving need to cleanse myself of sins. It's because I need to get rid of what I brought to this plane."

``And where is the Demon now?" Esmarelda asked.

"That's part of the problem. A few years later, I lured it to Detroit and trapped it under Hart Plaza with a series of sigils and a little help from my friends. I needed the nickel because it was the backdoor." I pointed a finger at Esmeralda "Always keep a backdoor in case you need it".

"I know all about that, my friend." Esmarelda said.

"I guess you do." I laughed. "So this place, this 510 Leith St, has the ghosts of Faust's dad and kid sister and well as echoes of that bastard entity that possessed Dorian."

"Do you know what it was?" Es asked, "That took Dorian"

"Yeah." I paused "you got a smoke?" I asked Es. She pulled out a djarum and lit it for me. "Thanks." I took a long drag. "It was the Dark Star."

"You have got to be fucking me." Esmarelda said.

"I wish that were the case." I said, looking out the window.

"We can arrange that." Esmarelda said with a smirk.

"In time." I said. "But first, we need to talk to someone."

"Fine. Who?" She asked.

"Amy Lenkner." I answered.

'Who is that?" Esmarelda asked

"The second vessel." I uttered. "She used to live off of Academy."

"Let's do this. I got nothing but time and an unrelenting hatred of possessing entities." Esmarelda chided.

"That's the ticket," I said.

I pointed Esmarelda in a direction and headed off toward the Lenkner house.

"So, did you fuck her?" Esmarelda asked as we drove.

"Nope." I replied.

"Did you want to fuck her?" Es asked. I did not reply. "Got it," Esmarelda replied and resumed attention on driving.

I felt a buzz in my pocket. I reached in my coat pocket to check my phone. Unknown number. I have a general rule, when it comes to numbers I don't recognize. If it doesn't come up with Angelic script on my caller ID, I have no interest. Leave a voicemail like everyone else.

"Who was it?" Esmarelda asked.

"I don't know. Some fucker keeps trying to call every since we got into town." I answered.

"Did they leave a message?" She asked, audibly irritated.

"Yeah, but I didn't listen to them." I replied.

"Why the fuck not?" She asked.

"Just not important to me." I answered.

"You have literally no way of knowing if it is important or not without listening to the message, jackass. So listen." She commanded.

"Fine" I replied. I listened to the voicemail. I belted out a maniacal cackle. "The fuck!??" I said to Esmarelda.

"Now this, I can tell, is going to be good." Esmarelda commented.

Chapter 9: The Call

"I cannot fucking believe this." I said. "Just un-fucking-believeable"

"I'm waiting." Esmarelda said impatiently

"Okay, just bear with me. This is going to take some backstory." I said. "So I knew this guy in high school, His name was Ivan. Ivan was the kid that everyone knew but no one really admitted to knowing. Big time theatre nerd. Ironically a good friend of Amy Lenkner."

"I follow so far." She replied.

"We haven't talked in a few years. Like twenty years." I said

"Was that him?" She asked.

"Yeah." I answered.

"And?" She asked.

"Oh. Right. He was trying to sell me a harpsichord." I replied.

"I feel like I missed something." Esmarelda stated with her head cocked.

"Me too." I said

"No. Really." Esmarelda insisted. "There has to be some link in that chain of thought."

"Fuck it. I'm gonna call him back." I said impulsively

"How are you going to do that, genius?" Esmarelda chided.

"He left his number in the voicemail. Duh." I snickered.

"Fine" She snipped.

I dialed the numbers. "It's ringing" I said to Esma

"Congrats on mastery of basic technology" Esmarelda quipped

"Fu...oh hey Ivan." I spoke into the phone. "I got your message. What's up?"

"Oh hi Neil." Without a pause he dove right into it. "Long story short, I have this harpsichord for sale. It's really nice. It's all black, with white accidentals. Very gently used."

"I'm gonna stop you there, Ivan. I have no use for a harpsichord." I interjected.

A long pause on the other end of the line. "Well. It's really nice. And I could let it go for cheap. Um...like Five Thousand." He queried.

I laughed a hearty belly laugh. "You have GOT to be fucking putting me on! When was the last time we talked? Like the summer after college?" I asked Ivan.

"You don't have to be rude. Let's just get together and discuss the terms of the sale." Ivan pushed.

"There are no terms of the sale. You fucking cold called me. And how the fuck did you even get this number?" I asked

"You gave it to me," Ivan answered.

Shit. I may have. "Well either way, I don't need a harpsichord and I don't have five grand." I said.

"Fine. I guess I'll just check with someone else." Ivan said and ended the call.

Esmarelda both sat in stunned silence.

"Ever think maybe I wanted a harpsichord?" Esmarelda asked.

I looked at her, unsure quite what to say. After a few moments, She broke into raucous laughter. Yeah, that's what I thought was happening here. "But seriously, we could have used his..." Esmarelda's speech devolved into gasps of laughter. "Okay, okay, I'm done."

"Are you sure?" I asked.

"No, I'm not done." She replied through fits of laughter. We pulled up to the Lenkner place. "Okay. That was a good laugh. And are you sure that harpsichord wasn't code for something?" She asked.

"I try to be as sure of little as possible." I answered.

"How's that working out for you?" She jabbed.

I gave her a dirty look.

"What's your plan?" Esmeralda inquired.

"Do I look like someone with a plan?" I asked.

"Not really." Esmarelda answered. "You just going to knock on the door at 2 am and expect it to go well for you?"

"This is Brighton. I'm not likely to get shot for knocking on a door." I said.

"Because you're white." She replied.

"Fair enough," I replied.

I exited Merideth and walked to the front stoop. I knocked on the door. No answer. I waited and knocked again. I heard a yell from the other side of the door.

"I've got a twelve gauge in my hand and don't give a shit about my front door. I suggest you leave."

That was a man's voice. I really hope I have the right house was my thought.

"Look, I'm just looking for Aimee. Do you know Aimee?" I yelled through the door.

"One..." The man shouted.

"Why are you counting?" I asked nervously

"Two...you got till Five. Then I cut you in half." the man called.

"Shit. I'm sorry, man. I just have some serious business with

Aimee" I said.

'Serious enough to die about? Three...God damn Cultists need to stop coming around here. She's out!" The man yelled.

Oh shit. The Hallow. I thought that was done with. Having all I needed, I called out to the man on the other side of the door with my hands raised. "Okay, okay. I'm leaving. Just tell her Hawthorne stopped by."

I heard the deadbolt disengage. I took three big steps back. The door slowly creaked open. "Neil?" The squat, shotgun wielding man in a tank top and boxer shorts called to me, puzzled.

"Um. Yeah. Neil Hawthorne. I'm an old friend of Aimee's from high school, sorry for the bother." I said apologetically.

"You don't recognize me, do you?" The man asked.

"Can't say as I do, but I don't have great night vision these days. Getting old is a bitch." I chuckled.

"It's Carl," He said, shotgun now at his side.

"Oh, shit! Carl? Yeah so, you and Aimee, huh?" I said.

"Come in before somebody calls the cops." Carl opened the door for me.

"Um. My um. My girlfriend is in the car" I said somewhere between a statement and a question.

"I'm not your girlfriend!" I heard Esmarelda yell from the car.

"She'll be fine in the car." I said to Carl. I followed him inside. I did not remember Carl, but I was just rolling with it.

I walked inside the house, into the foyer. Carl motioned for me to sit in the living room.

"I'll go upstairs and get Aimee". Carl climbed the stairs.

I looked around the room. It was a standard Brighton place. A lot of photos of people that I didn't recognize. A lot of family photos. Vacations. Christmas get-togethers. All of the trappings of a life the type of which I never led. It gave me a glimpse into how things could have been if I had stayed in Brighton and settled down instead leading this life of glamor and excitement that I chose. Don't get me wrong, I have saved the world a dozen times over, but there is something about the everyday glory of a life more well contained. A life of domesticity. Then again, I probably would have shot myself in the face long before I got to be this age.

"Neil?" I heard a call from the stairs. At the top of the staircase standing in a housecoat was the twenty plus year aged artifact of Aimee Lenkner. "I thought you were dead."

"Well I was for a little, but I got better." I replied with a smirk.

"So, you and Carl, huh?" I asked.

"Yeah. We've been married fifteen years now." Aimee replied. "You probably don't remember him. No one seems to remember him. He was the captain of the QuizBowl team when we were in High School. Does that help?" Aimee asked.

I still had no idea who Carl was. Being aware of my limitations, I wasn't overly concerned that I didn't remember Carl, as there are probably as many people I've forgotten as I've met, but that fact that no one remembered him did make me a bit nervous. "Yeah, that sounds about right." I replied. Nothing was right about that. It was about then that I spotted something that may be of some help.

"Where are my manners, Neil? Would you like me to put on some coffee?" Aimee asked.

"Sure. I could go for some coffee." I answered.

Aimee excused herself to the kitchen, to what I had presumed was to make some coffee as she had mentioned.

Becoming suddenly aware of his state of undress, Carl became self-conscious. "Oh. Hey. I'm gonna go put some clothes on". Carl ventured up the stairs to get dressed.

"I hope you're good with Instant." Aimme said as she returned from the kitchen.

"That's just grand." I answered. I made a cheesy gesture as I raised the mug to my lips as if to say, damn that's good stuff. I was lying. I could not then nor can I now stand instant coffee. It is an abomination and should be destroyed. The subterfuge was sufficient to fool my host. I lowered my voice. "Look, Aimes. I need to ask you something before your beau gets back. Do you remember that shit that went down with Dorian Faust?"

She dropped her coffee cup, sending shards of ceramic and shitty coffee spilling hither and yon over the department store throw rug. The blanching of her face was all the confirmation I needed.

"Everything okay down there?" Carl called from upstairs.

I gave Aimee a stern eye. "Everything will be fine. I just need to see your necklace" I pointed to the necklace around her neck. I motioned my hand over Aimee's face. "Tell him everything is fine."

"Everything's fine." Aimee spoke in a monotone. She unclasped the chain from her neck and handed it to me. I took the chain and the charm on it and held it in my right hand. With it, a flood of images came to me.

I saw the house on Leith. I saw Dorian being tortured in that botched bullshit excuse for an exorcism, despite Aimee not being there when it happened. I saw the Dark Star leaving his body and drifting through a gate into Aimee's body. I saw through her eyes how she had been possessed and the feeling of being trapped within her own skin. I saw after she was freed of the malady and how that ratfuck Doro lured it into a gate. Even a broken clock is right twice a day, I guess. With Doro it was more like once by my account.

I saw images of the time after. I felt the scar that Aimee had kept on her psyche much like the same tear that Faust has to this day. I saw how she met Carl and I saw the harassment by the Hallow Cult. I broke out of my trance with the sound of Carl's heavy footfalls down the stairs. I set down the necklace. I took a sip of my instant bullshit coffee, trying not to gag.

"You got any bourbon, Carl?" I asked him as he descended the stairs.

"Yeah. A little nightcap sounds like a great idea." Aimee added.

Carl took a look at his wife. "Honey? You alright? You look like you've seen a ghost."

"Yeah. I...I'm fine. Just" She stammered. Digging deep into her bag of high school theatre tricks, she vamped. Aimee motioned at me.

"Neil just told me why he is in town."

Wondering what kind of bullshit she was going to dole out, I sipped my coffee. Aimee continued, "Neil's parents recently passed and he is here to sign off on the house. You see, Dear. Neil and his brother Roger have always had a contentious relationship." Aimee looked at me with a sympathetic posture.

I did my best to seem like a sad sack. "It's true. That's why I'm here at such an ungodly hour. I just didn't know where to turn. Aimes was the last tie I had to this town." I confirmed.

"Sorry to hear about your hard luck, friend." Carl consoled me.

"Thank" I replied. I stood and extended a hand to Carl. "I'm gonna get going. Sorry for the fright."

"What about the bourbon?" Carl asked.

"Oh. Right. I'm driving home." I doubled back.

"What about your girlfriend? Can't she drive?" Carl asked.

"If I come back stinking of spirits, I'm gonna hear about it." I said.

"Understood. Keep that lady happy. She sounds like a keeper." Carl said jovially.

"Yeah. Sure thing." I replied. I gave Aimee a hug and she walked me to the door. I slipped one of my business cards into Aimee's housecoat pocket. "call me." I whispered into her ear as she embraced me. When she let me go, she nodded.

"Ok Neil. Best of luck with the estate." Aimee said.

"I think I'm gonna need it." I replied and walked out the front door.

I let myself into Meredith. Esmarelda turned to me and motioned widely with her arms. "Well? What took so long?" Esmarelda asked,

"We had a lot of ground to cover." I answered.

"So didja fuck her?" Esmarelda asked sharply.

"You have a one track mind, my dear." I laughed. "No. I did not."

"Good. She looked hideous." Es confided.

"That was her husband at the door." I replied.

"That explains a thing or seven." Es was relieved. "Let's get." We sped off toward town center. "What's next?"

"I got one more stop." I replied. "Old Town Hall."

"I'm gonna need some direction here." Es replied.

"Just sniff for the nearest Doomsday Cult." I replied.

"So it's like that, huh?" She asked.

'It's like that indeed." I answered.

Chapter 10: The Hallow Cult

When I was a kid, we had a problem with a cult of so-called Satanists here in Brighton. They weren't actually Satanists. The good Christian folk of the jewel of Livingston county saw a few destructive acts and a few murdered pets and automatically conflated that with the work of the Devil. I've met the Devil. He doesn't have any interest in any of that horseshit.

There was a credible, albiet mislabeled, threat to the safety of the greater community and meanwhile the church ladies and PTO head were trying to get kids barred from playing Dungeons and Dragons for the same stupid reasons. As always, those in power fear what they don't understand or what they can't control. The Hallow Cult, as they called themselves, were nothing more than a gang of misinthropes who liked to set small fires, smoke a lot of pot, and instill fear in people so they got left the fuck alone. Their plan backfired and resulted in the strictest curfew the town had ever known.

After the appearance of the Dark Star in 1994, the Hallow gained an actual degree of supernatural power. The Dark Star, being a creature of pure corruption, was inclined toward pulling those that were already headed that way on an express slide to total bedlam chaos. None of it amounted to much. Most of it was just preternatural strength and endurance, but when you're going toe to toe with the crazy bastards it's hard to down play.

Their headquarters was a secret room underneath Old Town Hall. Old Town Hall was finished being built in 1879. Back then there used to be a lot of underground storage that is no longer used. One of the sub cellars was walled off, but the Cult figured out how to access it from a tunnel leading behind the Mill Pond.

When we got to the Old Town Hall, I motioned for Es to park along Main Street near the Mill Pond. She cut the engine.

"So what's the plan?" Es asked "Go in both guns blazing?"

"You have guns?" I asked.

"Sadly, no" She answered. "Fuck it. We don't need em"

"As much as I hate those bastards, I don't think killing a bunch of teenage punks is going to improve our situation. I need to get something from their lair." I replied.

"What's that?" She asked.

"It's stupid." I paused. "But they have this artifact under there."

"You're shitting me." She said.

"Yeah. It's an ebony cross." I said.

"You have my attention." Esmarelda said with excitement.

"Alright. We do this" I affirmed.

We left the Caddy parked on the street, and popped the trunk. I pulled the all or nothing (TM) bag from the trunk. Esmarelda gave me a sassy look. I nodded approval at her interest. I opened the backpack, produced two bundles of rope and two miniature squirt guns.

"Is that what I think it is?" Esmarelda asked.

"Of course it is." I replied.

"Of course it is." She nodded. She took one of the squirt guns and held it at the ready.

We both threw the ropes around our shoulder. I threw the All or Nothing on my other shoulder and we crept down the tunnel. Knowing what to look for, we effortlessly found our way into the Hallow Lair.

The exterior of the Lair dictated it could not be more than a few feet in length. However, on the inside, the vault extended thirty feet and was about ten feet deep. There was an altar at the end of the vault that was constructed from animal bones and had the Black Cross setting inside it.

"Is that *THE* black cross?" Es asked.

"It's *A* black cross." I answered.

"But probably not *THE* Black Cross?" She pressed.

"I have given up on the idea of surprise as well as the notion of hope. But if there is a chance that it could be *THE* Black Cross, I have all kinds of ideas for that son of a bitch." I qualified

"Agreed." Esmarleda took a few steps toward the altar.

Stepping from out of the shadows were three robed figures.

"Fuck." I whispered.

"To what do we owe the pleasure?" Asked one of the Cultists. "We don't get too many visitors"

"I'm not gonna bulshit you, friendo." I said. "I need that cross from your altar there."

The two cultists on the flanks grabbed for the scimitars hanging from their belts.

"I'm afraid we can't allow that, *friendo*." The middle Cultist chided.

"I wasn't askin" I clarified.

"We aren't negotiating" The middle cultist countered.

"Look, fuckers" Es interrupted. "We're leaving with that Fucking Cross. Capice?"

"We have a different opinion on the topic, miss" The leader stated. The two flanking cultists advanced.

"Stop right there." Es commanded, drawing her water pistol.

"I'm afraid you're going to need more than that, my dear." The leader laughed. The two cultists brandished their scimitars and charged Es. She lept back and shot them both in the face with a stream of water. The cultists fell to their knees, dropping their blades and clutching their faces.

"Holy Water, I presume." The Cult Leader asked.

"Better." I replied. "It's the Blood of the Mother."

The Cult Leader's face flattened. He suddenly and clearly knew what he was up against. See, the Blood of the Mother was something that magicians in the area used to refer to water from Lake Superior. In the metaphysical structure of the great lakes, there is nothing as sacred as water from the Greatest of the Great Lakes. She is Mother, and her water is the Blood of Creation. There are those that believe that Michigan is where the world began. Who am I to say that is wrong? Either way, the water had power over these rat bastard misanthropes and Culty Boi knew that. He wasn't prepared to take his chances.

"Take it" The Cult Leader said. "The cross is nothing but charred wood. You will find it quite useless in whatever endeavor you are attempting. It is literally garbage."

"One man's trash is another man's spell component." I quipped.

Esmarelda kept her pistol trained on the Leader. I walked behind her and moved toward the altar. The Cult Leader maintained eye contact with Esmarelda the entire time.

"How did you know to find us here?" The Leader asked.

"You need to leave Aimee alone." I said to The Leader.

"We will do no such thing." He replied. "Now that it is known that there is a link between you, we will double our efforts. She is a sacred vessel of our dark master." The Leader was growing more impassioned as he spoke.

I turned to Es. "Would you do the honors?" I asked her.

"Gladly." Esmarelda replied. The pulled the trigger on her water pistol and a stream of Superior Water blasted out at the Leader. He attempted to move out of the way to no avail. His half goat head-dress was far too large and cumbersome. He was hit square on the chest with the Mother's Blood. Clutching at himself and screaming, he fell to the ground, expounding wails of agony.

"That's the trick." I said with glee.

Esmeralda ripped three more shots at the Leader, now causing his skin to burst into flame. "Shit." I exclaimed. I ran to the altar and grabbed the cross. We hauled ass out the tunnel as the unholy vestments within started to engulf in flame. By the time we reached the street, Old Town Hall had been completely taken over by the flames.

"Unplanned nicety" Esmarelda exclaimed. "Bonus points for me"

I adored her admiration for terrible ideas. We jumped in Meredith and lit off down Main Street. Two Fire Engines swung around the corner as we turned around Grand River Ave, making no observance of traffic law.

"I guess I can scratch 'burn down Brighton cultural icon' off of my list of things to do." I chuckled.

"It's not the outcome you desired, but it's the outcome you needed, Neil." Es justified.

"Indeed." I replied. "Indeed"

I threw the Black Cross in the All or Nothing Bag.

"Where to?" Esmarelda asked. "Only a few hours until sunrise and we turn back into etterkins. I mean PUMP-kins." She winked at me like she were in an old time matinee.

"We need to get some things sorted out. But we need to travel a lot faster than even old Meredith allows." I said.

"You askin what I think you're askin?" Es asked.

"You know I am." I replied.

Esmarelda stood on the accelerator. "Alright then." The El Dorado opened up all four chambers of its Internal Combustion Heart. With perfect fluid accuracy, she cut the wheel and made an impossible turn. Directly into a brick wall.

We passed through the wall and ended up on Woodward Avenue. Damn fairies get me every fucking time.

Chapter 11: Back to the D

Part I

The Sigil of Woe

We slowed considerably as we exited the gate, matching the speed of traffic on Woodward. We were downtown, near Campus Martius and in the vicinity of one of the sigils I constructed.

"Pull over in this alley" I motioned to a spot for Esmarelda to pull over. We exited Meredith and grabbed our things. I leaned in to the empty Cadillac and spoke, "You should probably just drive around while we handle business." I slammed the massive door and she backed out of the alley and proceeded down Woodward.

"So what about the getaway ride?" Esmarelda asked mischievously.

"Ain't no getting away." I answered far more stoically than was warranted. "We're in this until it's done."

"Understood." Esmeralda replied.

We walked back to Campus Martius. I led and Esmarelda followed, for a change. I stopped in the center of the courtyard. "This is it," I said.

"Do the thing, Neil. I believe in you." Esmarelda said with a wide smile. I was unaccustomed to this level of enthusiasm in areas in which it was appropriate. It seemed the only times she was really invested were in carnal delight or battling the otherworldly. She was Dark Fae after all, and I'm not sure she could do anything to shake that conditioning. I'm equally unsure that she would want to. I was curious whetehr this was eqauted more to fucking or fighting in her mind. I motioned up to a piece of statuary. "Right there. Can you see it?"

Esmarelda looked at the horseman. "Yep. Sign of Woe." She said. "What made you pick that one?" she asked.

"The thing I was binding had earned the pain I would inflict upon it." I answered.

"But that is a little far outside of standard operating procedure, even for a Necromancer. Endless torture is not something we encourage in our constitueency. What constitutes criteria for this battle framework? Willingness to subject others to torure in the main selling point." I concluded.

The eyes of the horse glowered as we approached. I pulled down the sigil and all sense of life left the stature. One down, four to go. No sooner did the statue lose it's glow, did I hear a low hum come from everywhere around us.

"What's that?" Esmarelda asked.

"Shit if I know." I answered.

"I don't plan to stick around and find out." Esmarelda replied

We started to flee the area. A great mist enveloped us from the ground. It was a whitish yellow smoke. It formed a pillar heading upward into the sky. At the end of the pillar, I saw an armored figure descending. It had a blue hue and was completely enclosed in metal.

"Professor! " I called out.

"You know this guy?" Ez asked

"I know of him. We've worked in similar circles". I answered.

"Yeah. Ok". Esmarelda resigned and sat herself on a half wall.

The Professor turned his attention to me. His metallic voice rang out. "You've disturbed my Sigil. State your name"

"First of all, it's my sigil. Second of all, were you assigned by someone to guard this? Because you did a shit job" I chastised.

Esmarelda chuckled, "Nice".

"You must be the Necromancer," the Professor announced.

"Yeppers" I answered.

"You sure know how to make an entrance," Esmarelda added. "aren't you worried about attracting attention?"

"As flashy as I am, no one sees me" the Professor confided. "I'm surprised the both of you saw me, to be honest"

"We're special" she said with a smirk

"Indeed. We are special cases. Now back to business. Who put you here?". I asked

"I was assigned by Mother Superior, as all of us were. Did you not ever work for Project Delphi?"

"Yeah. I've been trying to forget it. It didn't end well" I

scoffed.

"What happened?" Esmarelda asked.

"A number of things on a number of realities. Basically we ended up fighting a world ending Mad Titan. That was the bullshit I got pulled into." I remarked

"Sounds unpleasant," Esmeralda remarked.

"Is that how you ended up being taken off the roster, dear man?" The professor asked.

"I had to use time travel to fix the problem. I do not like time travel." I said.

"I find it entirely unpleasant," the professor remarked. "But we've travelled afield from where we are intended. why did you deactivate the sigil?'

"Well. That's a bit of a long story to be honest. And I don't know that we actually have time to tell it. But I'll give it a shot." I took a breath deep enough to cast out the ridiculousness I was about to spew. "When I was a kid, I summoned a demon. That demon was allowed to run free and wreak havoc so long as it did what I wanted when I wanted it. In 2003, I imprisoned it under Hart Plaza. As part of the imprisonment, five sigils were cast to oversee the five elments of the binding: woe, agony, strife, loss, and retribution." I paused "do you know what I mean?"

"I believe so. But by removing a sigil, you are weakening the Beast's ability to be detained" the professor analyzed.

"Precisely" I answered

"Then why are you freeing it?" Professor asked

"I need a favor and it is the only creature that can supply that favor". I replied.

"In life we must sometimes make calculated risks for the good of all." The Professor stated. "You have my aid if you should need it"

"Well I appreciate that Professor. I'll have to get back to you." I replied. "Maybe give us a lift?"

"I think that can be arranged." He held both of his arms out to the sides. "Hop on" Esmarelda and I approached the Professor and clung to an arm each. With a sputter and a pop we took to the sky, spiralling through the Detroit night skyline.

Part II

The Sigil of Agony

I had the Professor drop Esmeralda and myself off at Central Station. I wasn't entirely sure how good an idea it was to return so soon to a place where I very nearly died, but what must be done, must right? Once we got settled on the ground, The Professor looked up at Central Station.

"Are you sure you don't need a helping hand, Sorcerer?" The Professor asked.

"I think between the two of us, we've got it licked, Prof" I answered.

"Suit yourself, friend. Should you need me, I am but a signal away." Professor told me and took off on a cloud of steam into the night, vanishing into the city skyline.

It was fitting that the site of the sigil of Agony was the very place that I got run over by a truck and faced down the Grim Reaper. Apparently my magicks are still working on some level, even just to hold in my greatest mistake. I looked to my left and noticed Esmeralda looking up at the defunct train station.

"This one's gonna hurt," I told Esmeralda.

"Wonderful" She replied. She turned back to me "Don't get me wrong, I'm down to get down. But why are you doing this again?"

I exhaled deeply to make room for the heavy words I was about to speak. "These sigils were put in place in order to seal the demon that I summoned when I was a little boy. I am taking the sigils down to release the demon."

"And why would you release a demon?" She asked.

"I made a mistake in imprisoning him and I need to undo it" I answered flatly.

"I can respect that. I think it's fucking stupid, but I can respect it." Esmeralda said. "So, what's the plan?"

"The sigil is located inside the floor of Central Station. We need to get inside. Then I need to undo the sigil." I said

"Sounds straightforward enough." She replied.

"One would think." I replied. "But based on what happened with the Professor at the Sigil of Woe, there is probably going to be some Delphi Asshole guarding it to make sure nothing happens to the sigil. The Professor is a man of logic and seeing as I made the damn thing, he wasn't going to kick the shit out of me for trying to undo it." I gulped. "Not everyone is going to be so understanding or flexible in their approach."

"I can be very persuasive, love." Esmeralda replied. "Leave the talking to me."

"I can't see what could go wrong." I replied. "Let's do this."

Esmarelda and I gathered up our wits, steeled our resolve, and made way for the security fence. We walked the perimeter for about three minutes until Ez lost her patience. "Fuck this" She said. She drew a rectangle on the chain link fence with her index finger. A section of fencing fell away with a clang. "After you, monsieur." Esmarelda did a half bow and motioned for me to walk ahead.

"Thanks, Lady Stealth" I laughed.

"Lady Stealth was on the B Team, right?" Esmarelda asked.

"I thought I made that up," I said.

"I'm pretty sure she's an actual superhero," Es replied.

"Your guess is as good as mine." I replied.

"Weren't you on the fucking team, Neil?" Esmarelda asked, growing increasingly more annoyed with my ignorance.

"One job. I did one job with those assholes. Now I keep getting junk mail from them. It's a list you cannot get removed from." I replied

"They send you junk mail?" Es asked.

"It was a metaphor," I said.

"I don't get your humor sometimes, Neil. Maybe you should just try not." Esmarelda advised.

"Probably a good plan." I affirmed.

We continued toward Central Station. The front door was wide open. We walked inside. Central Station had become a favored destination for tent cities as the station became defunct and construction was delayed due to difficulties with permits. The homeless people around looked nervously at the two of us.

"We need some cover," I said to Esmarelda.

She reached into her pocket and threw some glitter into the air. "That should do." She said.

'What the fuck was that?" I asked.

"Um. Fairy Dust." She said with disdain.

'Fairy dust?" I asked.

"Yeah. Did I fucking stutter?" She asked.

"It's just that." I said.

"It's just what Neil?" She asked.

"I just." I stuttered.

"Spill it, Hawthorne." She said bitingly.

"You never struck me as a fairy dust sort." I said.

"I got tricks you'll never see coming, Neil. By the way, speaking of unseen. We're invisible for the next ten minutes. You should make use of that." She cautioned.

"Right-o" I replied.

We moved undetected to the platforms. I found the sigil and started to make motion to undo it. I felt my hand held in the air.

"That's far enough, Necromancer." A voice spoke from the shadows.

"Who's there?" I called out. "And how can you see me?" I asked

"I can see your aura." The voice spoke. A figure stepped out from the shadows. A bald man standing about 5 feet tall and wearing the garb of a Shaolin monk.

"Mantis?" I asked.

"Yes, I am the one they call Mantis." He replied. "What

business have you here?"

"I am here to deactivate this sigil." I answered.

"I am aware of your intention, Sorcerer." Mantis stated calmly. "I do not know the reason why you are attempting this foolish task."

"I am responsible for illegally imprisoning an intelligent being. Freedom is warranted unless proven otherwise, don't you think?" I asked.

"The joy of making decisions about this particular duty is not mine." Mantis replied. "I was given a responsibility to maintain this sigil and that I shall. No matter what."

"And there is nothing I can say to persuade you then?" I asked, still held fast by Mantis's paralysis. "Hey by the way that is a pretty neat trick, keeping me held like this."

"I am beyond flattery, Mr. Hawthorne." Mantis said. "The Ego is the great trap of the human condition. I have been freed of that particular prison."

"Then you should appreciate what I am trying to do. I imprisoned an extraplanar creature against his will and I cannot bear that any longer. Please help me." I begged.

"I cannot abandon my station, Sorcerer. You just need to accept that." Mantis said.

"Hey, so why didn't the Countess know you were in town?" I asked.

"How do you mean?" Mantis asked.

"I saw her earlier and she didn't mention you when I asked who was around." I clarified

"She is not aware that I am present. I am able to mask my presence from others using my discipline." Mantis said.

"So seeing as you are so disciplined and clearly possess superhuman abilities, you are well beyond my capabilities." I said. "What say you, we just sit and talk a bit?"

"I see no harm in that, Mr. Hawthorne." Mantis released me from my bonds. I fell away from the sigil.

"Ooof." I grunted as I fell to the floor. Mantis walked over to me to help me up. Once I was standing again, I resumed my conversation with Mantis. "So do you know the history of this place?" I asked.

"I know this place is a point of commerce. It was once a travel hub." Mantis replied

"A train station to be particular." I replied

"I believe you are correct." Mantis said.

"Do you believe in ghosts?" I asked.

"The energy pattern that is the human spirit expresses itself in many ways. One of which is as ghostly entities." Mantis said.

"Ghosts love train stations." I said. "Something about being a waypoint. Spirits transitioning from our world to the next. Trains are a nice metaphor for that."

"That fits nicely." Mantis agreed.

"I picked this place to set the Sigil of Agony because there is so much spiritual movement through this area." I said.

"How does that affect the sigil?" Mantis asked.

"Because of the constant flow of spiritual energy, it can be hard to sense certain auras. Even for the most developed mind." I said,

Her eyes narrowed. She began to enter a defensive physical stance. "I do believe you have tricked me, Sorcerer. But what you do not know is that I, Mantis am the Guardian of the Undying Flame of…."

A large segment of the ceiling collapsed on Mantis's head. I was sent tumbling back to the platform where the sigil stood. I looked back and noted that Mantis was struggling beneath the wreckage but what was not killed. I breathed a sigh of relief. I began deconstructing the sigil. When my hands touched the pattern, a wave of pain shot through me. Not pain so much as Agony. The sigil was its own defence.

I fought through, digging deep into my training. I dissociated myself from my physical body in order to move through the pain. A moment later, the sigil was deactivated. Right about the time Mantis was freeing herself from the pile of debris. She rose from the pile covered in a translucent green flame. I reconnected with my corporeal form.

"I need you to really hear me, Mantis, Guardian of the Whatever" I spouted off.

"The Undying Flame of Shangri-La!" Mantis shouted. She charged at me.

I knew at that point my Agony was only beginning. Mantis struck me with blinding speed and impossible accuracy. She manipulated my chakras into a feedback loop of pain. I crumpled to the floor in a ball, unable to do anything but writhe in burning suffering. The pain was so intense that I couldn't even enter into my astral form. I was locked in. Beyond the haze of neurologic and energetic disruption I heard a shrill whistle come from the shadows.

"Yo, Bitch!" Esmarelda yelled out. "Nice hairdo" Esmarelda now allowed herself to be seen. "I'm gonna need you to cease and desist all combative action against my friend."

"The Sorcerer needs to be taught an important lesson. He must be made to suffer for his arrogance." Mantis spoke.

"And it's your job to punish him, eh?" Esmarelda asked pointedly.

"It is my task to guard this sigil. As if it were my temple." Mantis clarified.

"How enlightened of you to make a mortal man suffer for your own delight." Esmarelda taunted.

"I take no pleasure in this. I suffer with him. It is for the good of all that I do this." Mantis replied.

"How about you let me fight you to settle this?" Esmarelda asked.

"Fight? Me?" Mantis asked.

"Well. It's clear you understand english." Esmarelda chided.

"Now what about my offer?"

"If I face you in combat, I will not offer any quarter. You understand that plain english, don't you?" Mantis asked.

"I would not ask any." Esmarelda replied.

"Then the accord is struck." Mantis entered into a ready pose. "We begin now." Mantis rushed at Esmeralda, fists and feet swinging in blinding fury. No blow was able to be landed. Just when it seemed one would, Es effortlessly moved away from the strike.

"Is that the best you have?" Esmarelda asked Mantis.

"How is this possible?" The Monk became enraged. Long sequestered emotion overcame Mantis. Her movements became erratic and sloppy. Esmarelda started to smile.

"You're allowing yourself to feel and have given in to your own demons, Mantis" Esmarelda chided.

Mantis finally landed a blow on Esmarelda. Directly across the face with a backfist. Esmarelda was sent tumbling to the ground. As much mystic fire and training as there was, all Esmarelda felt was the hate. Mantis fell to her knees and wept.

"What have you done?" Mantis whispered, letting the sheath of flame recede.

"I found your weakness and exploited it. Nothing more." Esmarelda explained.

"You've ruined me." Mantis sobbed.

Esmarelda walked to Mantis and offered a hand out. "Stand" She commanded.

Mantis took Esmarelda's hand and stood. "What use am I?" Mantis asked.

"You need to get out of your own way. Just like you did all those years ago. You must surrender." Esmarelda instructed.

Mantis embraced Esmarelda. "Thank you" She whispered in Esmarelda's ear. "You've taught me an important lesson this day." She broke the embrace and bowed. Mantis then disappeared into a green pillar of fire.

"Alright, Neil. Time to get up." Esmarelda commanded. "Enough fooling around. We've got work to do."

I got up, dusted myself off and proceeded away from what was left of Central Station. Back to the street, we met with Meredith, climbed in and headed away.

"What's next?" Esmarelda asked.

"The next sigil is Strife. It is located nearby the Fox Theatre." I answered.

"Lovely, darling. I don't think I'm dressed for a show unfortunately." Esmarelda mused.

"You're dressed just for where we are headed." I said with a smirk.

Part III

The Sigil of Strife

We pulled up next to the Fox and headed around back. Meredith let us out and sped away. The area around the Fox was always teeming with humanity. It was the theatre district as well as adjacent to Comerica Field, Ford Stadium and the newly minted Little Ceasar's arena. I looked about with a mixture of awe and heartbreak.

"What gives?" Esmarelda asked.

"Last time I was here, none of these arenas were a thing." I extolled.

"How's that?" She asked.

"The Fox has been here since forever, but all this shit over here." I motioned across the street to the stadiums. "None of that bullshit was here. Not that I was a big sports fan, but when I was a kid the Tigers played at a place called...get this...Tiger's Stadium. And it was over on Trumbull." I concluded.

"Gee Neil, thanks for the triptych, but unless that information has fuckall to do with the location of the next sigil, I would recommend saving that for another time." Es requested.

"Fair enough" I agreed. "The sigil is in this alley". Esmarelda was at the ready. "Right back here" I motioned. Esmarelda ducked down the alley I motioned to. I followed close behind. "Fuck" I said under my breath.

"What's wrong?" Esmarelda asked, a growing annoyance in her voice.

"They must have built a new wall or something. It's not here." I replied.

"Maybe you just got it twisted. It's been a while, right?" She prompted.

"Yeah, but not THAT long. I don't understand, it should be right here." I said quizzically.

"Need me to smash some shit?" Esmarelda asked. I looked at her and she was holding a comically oversized crescent wrench.

"That's going to come in handy," I laughed. "But not right yet." I felt along the wall. "Here we go" I found the crevice. Apparently I had built a sliding passage. THAT was the part I had failed to remember. The wall slid away to reveal the sigil. "B-I-N-G-O" I spelled out.

"If the pattern holds, we should have someone crawling up our ass in a second. So do your thing, Necro-Boy. I got your back." Esmarelda offered.

"Alright. I got this" I turned back to the sigil, or rather what should have been the sigil. Standing interposing between myself and my destination was a pile of discarded junk. "I know I didn't just look through a pile of old transistor radios before." I turned to Esmarelda. "Did you just toss some old electronic junk in front of me?" I asked.

"What nonsense are you spreading?" Es asked.

My answer would become obviated by the pile of electronic junk whirring around in a cyclone around me. I did not have a good feeling about this. The refugee horde from Radio Shack continued to whirr about, slowly forming into a vaguely humanoid shape.

"State your purpose." The collection of discarded junk directed at me in a metallic shrill tone.

"I am Neil Hawthorne, Necromancer and former Sorcerer Supreme. I have come to take down the sigil behind you." I announced.

"I cannot allow that action" The machine-man opposed me.

"We weren't asking." Esmarelda shouted.

"Let's not act hastily," I said. "After all, if it were going to attack it probably would." The machine man did not respond. "What's YOUR name?" I asked.

"I am the Harbinger X-1. I am here to guard this sigil" the Harbinger said.

"We have to have some way to find a mutually beneficial answer to this scenario." I said.

"My assigned mission and your desired outcome do not intersect." Harbinger said. "Therefore I cannot allow you to destroy that which I am programmed to protect." It concluded.

"That clinches it then." I replied. "We have to go through you," I said.

"The probability of your success is low." Harbinger said.

"Don't tell me about probabilities." I scoffed. "There are an infinite number of timelines and in each of them every possible variation of events. You are tied to this single timeline. I exist throughout the infinite."

"I will not be bent to your tricks, Sorcerer. I am not an organic lifeform. Your magicks will be useless against me." Harbinger replied.

"You underestimate me, Harbinger." I scolded. "This is your last chance to surrender." I issued the ultimatum.

"Prepare to die in your infiniteness" Harbinger said. I think it may have been making a joke, but I never got robot humor. A missile launcher formed on its chest and it started to glow.

"Es" I said calmly.

"Got it," She replied. A bolt of lightning peeled out from the clear night sky. The electric arc shot through the machine, sending it into convulsions. The convulsions gave way to sparks and ultimately disassembly. The parts fell to the ground, inert.

"Thank you" I said to Esmarelda.

"Plenty of time for that later. I'm sure the effect is temporary. Do the thing" She commanded.

I stepped over the smoldering pile of circuitry and deactivated the sigil. "Okay, let's get the fuck outta here before it wakes up with a hell of a headache."

"Do robots get headaches?" Esmarelda asked.

"If they can, it will." I said with a half smile.

We exited the alley to be met by Meredith. She scooped us up and we sped away.

Part IV

The Sigil of Loss

The next stop was in a region of town called GreekTown. Most of GreekTown had been incorporated into being either directly part of or adjacent to the GreekTown Casino. I found this particularly fitting given the nature of the sigil. No kind of establishment better exemplifies loss than a casino. After all, the house always wins.

"The sigil is in a casino?" Esmarelda asked.

"No. The casino was built on top of the sigil. The draw of Loss was so strong that the area eventually became a drain on economic resources." I replied.

"So you made this happen, more or less?" She asked.

"More or less." I replied.

"That makes you one hell of a magician, I'd say." Esmarelda said.

"A magician makes change in accordance with their will. This is not my will." I replied.

"I know you know better than that.   It is change in accordance with THE Will.   Not YOUR will.   Noob." Esmarelda chided.

"Of course I knew that." I just was trying to bullshit her. I didn't know that she knew that.

Therein lay the rub.

We parked Meredith on the fifth floor of the parking garage. We exited the vehicle and made our way to the elevator. I pushed the button and we waited. I felt Esmarelda's hand brush against my thigh. She gripped my hand. I looked down at my hand and back up at her. Esmarelda's eyes remained fixed on the elevator door.

"I'm worried, Neil." Esmarelda confessed.

"What's the trouble, bubble?" I asked with a smirk.

"Look. I'm not being a baby, here. Don't talk to me like that." Esmarelda chided.   She did not remove her hand from mine, however.

"So what's eating you?" I inquired.

The elevator dinged and the door opened.

"Never mind. Let's go." Esmarelda led me into the awaiting elevator car. There were three casino goers, seemingly unrelated. We kept our hands held as the door shut. Esmarelda snuggled herself against me and placed my arm around her shoulder. She whispered something into my chest that was inaudible to me. A few minutes later, the door opened. Our three ride partners left the car. Esmarelda looked up at me and smiled. She gave me a quick peck on the lips and exited the elevator.

We walked into the casino.

"So...where are we headed here?" She asked.

"I'm kind of just following my gut here, but I think it is probably in the basement." I replied.

"Anything more specific than the basement?" She asked.

"It'll come to me in time." I replied.

"I'm on your timeline, chief." Es replied.

We passed through the main floor of the casino. Esmarelda would occasionally tap people playing slot machines on the shoulder, resulting in them hitting jackpots and progressives. Taking no responsibility for her role in the windfalls, she moved along effortlessly, asking no thanks for the gifts she was bestowing upon those in need. I looked on at her in awe. She did not act out of ego or self-promotion. Her actions were entirely altruistic. It was a level of love for others that I doubt I would ever attain.On reaching the elevators, Esmarelda turned to me.

"Is this the way down?" She asked.

"Not this way." I replied.

"We're going to have to use a different route then?" She asked.

"It would appear." I answered.

"DO you have a direct impression of where the sigil is yet, or are you still wandering in a fog?" Esmarelda asked.

"It's getting clearer." I replied.

"Let's work with that." Esmarelda took my face in her hands and caressed my cheek. "Kiss me, you animal." Esmarelda and I touched lips. I felt fire moving between us. We locked mouths passionately, exchanging energy and spit for what seemed like hours. Casino goers passed by us in uncomfortable, slow shuffling gaits. There are those that wished to escape our display of true lust, others that wished to somehow touch that forbidden flame. After we had reached the peak of our energies, we expelled them into the cosmos. She disengaged and broke the spell.

"I know where we are going now." I said, out of breath.

"Then let's get there." She said, letting out a satisfied sigh.

We walked down a series of hallways to the backstage of the Casino. To those uninitiated, casinos have what they call a frontstage, the place where the customers are, and a backstage, the place where the behind the scenes operations function. It's a thing that they perfected at Disney World. A lot of things are like that now, museums, casinos, hospitals even. A series of back doors and hallways that no one ever sees but the insiders. Kind of like magic in that regard. Or politics.

We reached a security door.

"Shit" I said. "We can't pass this."

"Can't?" Esmarelda asked with a haughty laugh. "Or won't?"

"Are you mocking me?" I asked playfully.

"No." She replied. "But I am challenging you" She let out a sly smile.

I placed my hands on the keypad. I tried a few tricks I had learned to no avail. "I am worried that I am going to trigger some kind of alarm if I try too many times."

"Let me try." Es said. "I have something of a talent with doors." She said with a smirk.

Esmarelda listened closely to the door, then sniffed the lock.

"What the actual…" I asked.

Esmarelda held up a single finger. Not the finger I was expecting either, she held up the index. I stopped talking and resumed observing her work. Esmarelda whispered something into the lock. A few sparks lept from her tongue. The keypad let out a few beeps and the door gently swung open.

A stood silently looking at Esmeralda.

"Well." She said, motioning to the door. "What are you waiting on? An engraved invitation?"

I shook out of my awe. I walked through the doorway that Ez had made available to me. Esmarelda followed close behind, keeping an eye to the path behind us.

The hallway stretched out before us, was grey and austere. It was free of the ostentatious allure of the rest of the hotel casino. This was an area that was clearly not meant for public access. I guess that could have been ascertained from the high level unpickable key press access point.

I could feel the sigil stronger than ever. There must have been some kind of containment ward on that door, keeping prying minds from tracking down the location of the sigil. Despite that fact, we were hot on its trail. I led Esmarelda to a set of stairs leading down into seemingly nothingness. I looked down to confirm.

"That's it. That's the way we go." I said, looking down.

"Look at me, Neil." Esmarelda spoke in a small, demure voice.

I complied, Looking her straight in the eyes.

"That is not a path that leads anywhere." Esmarelda said gently. "That is a hole in the fucking fabric of the cosmos" As her speech completed ending, her annoyance with my clearly idiotic plan was coming to the surface.

"I know how this looks." I replied.

"I don't think you do. It looks like you're either an idiot or completely fucking crazy." Esmarelda stated. "And seeing as I know you aren't an idiot." Es paused. "When did you lose your marbles?"

"This is a gateway to the Shadow Dimension." I clarified.

"I know what it is. Thanks for 'splaining it to little old me" Esmarelda reached into her coat and pulled out a length of gossamer thread.

"Where did you get that?" I asked.

She stopped and looked at me, her annoyance now unable to be contained. She started tying the strand to a railing. "If we are going into the Nether, we need a way to get back." Completing the knot, she handed me the loose end. "This will be just that."

"The Shadow Dimension operates very differently from this dimension, Es." I began to explain. Esmarelda placed one of her long black nailed fingers across my lips, and shushed me. "You can save your metaphysical dick waving. I don't need a dissertation on the nature of dimensional travel. I've been around." She concluded.

"I didn't mean to insult you." I apologized.

"I'm just a little keyed up. Kiss me." Esmarelda requested.

I pressed my face to hers, obeying her wish.

"Better?" I asked.

"Mmmm. Better." She purred.

Okay then. Shall we?" I asked, gripping the rope.

Esmarelda threw her arm around my shoulders and her legs around my hips. "Lets"

I lept. We dove feet first into oblivion.

As we crossed through the dimensional aperture, the air became thick and harder to breathe. The rope in my hand was the only illumination. I could see the well concealed terror in the corners of Esmarelda's expression. She is very good at keeping it tucked in, but as close as we've gotten, and the special bond we have shared, emotions became as plain as trigonometry. In other words obvious if you know what you're looking at.

We reached a floor of sorts. Our descent came to a slow stop and we were able to stand.

"Just leave the rope hanging there," Esmarelda told me. She pulled a ring out of a pouch on her belt. It glowed with a sense of calm and sincerity. I eyed it curiously. "Oh this old thing?" Esmeralda said coyly. "This was a gift from my mother. She got it from Queen Mab when she worked in the Courts"

"You're just full of surprises, aren't you?" I giggled.

"If I weren't, you'd be pretty well fucked." Esmarelda replied.

"Well, you aren't wrong." I replied.

We ventured deeper into the spongy inkwell that was the Shadow Dimension. As we passed further from the Earth Dimension, the alien nature of the realm became more and more apparent. In time, the inky black gave way to a clearing. A vague notion of the spectrum of visible light was emanating from a building in the distance. I knew at once what this was.

"The Crystal Palace." Esmarelda whispered.

Apparently I wasn't the only one who knew.

We approached the Crystal Palace. At this point, we were no longer walking, but lazily floating on some sort of spectral wind. The current took us to the drawbridge leading to the palace. As we approached the structure, it became more visible and what was once a suggestion of a glow had given way to a brilliance.

The Crystal Palace was seemingly hundreds of feet tall with an impossibly narrow spire in the center. The palace itself was resting atop a massive island that was floating suspended in the vast nothingness. A mechination whirred around the spire, with several orbs that seemed tiny from where we stood. In reality, the orbs were likely massive but we were so far away that they only seemed tiny.

Stepping out of the Void, a figure appeared before us. The figure was dressed in armor and held a halberd. It's dress was a variation on the Swiss Guard at the Vatican, with the purple traded for White and the Gold traded for Black. He held the halberd across our path.

"State your business." The Guard spoke

"We seek an audience with the Prince of Shade." I replied. Esmarelda, in a rare turn of events, stood silently.

"The Lord does not accept the audience at this time." The Guard replied.

"We are not expected, but we are welcome." I assured the Guard.

"Unfortunately I cannot simply accept your word on this. I have strict orders" The Guard stood his ground.

"I am Neil Hawthorne." I stated.

"And?" The Guard replied.

I could feel Esmarelda rolling her eyes.

"The Prince knows me." I clarified.

"I'm sure he does," the Guard replied. "But I cannot allow

you into the castle."

I pulled a fist sized gemstone from my pocket. It was pure black and cut at severe, incongruent angles. "I have tribute"

The Guard looked at the gem. His demeanor was changed. "Is that what I think it is?" He asked.

"Yes" I replied.

"I apologize for the delay. Please enter." The Guard called down the drawbridge. Esmarelda and I crossed the drawbridge into the Crystal Palace. We were met on the other side by two more identical guards with sabres on their belts. They led us in, past the portcullis into the main throne room. Sitting on the Crystal Throne was a white robed figure with a silver headdress. The rest of the robed figure was absolute darkness except for its two piercing triangular white eyes.

The robed figure raised an arm. The guards left the throne room. I bowed my head in deference. I nudged Esmarelda, and she acted in kind, bowing her head slightly and briefly.

"Prince of Shade, Lord Darkmarr, I offer you tribute." I

announced and held aloft the massive gemstone.

A voice, hollow and projecting from all sides, rung out. "Sorcerer Neil Hawthorne of Earth. It has been a very long time since I have seen you."

"Indeed it has been, Lord." I replied. "But do you really need to uphold this charade?"

The hollow voice let out a groan, "Fine. Rob me of my one joy in this existence." Darkmarr spoke. "What can I do for you, Neil?"

"I have the Heart of Darkness. I wish to exchange it for deactivating the Sigil of Loss."

"That is not a barter I can enter into lightly." Darkmarr replied. "Do you know what you are doing?" He asked.

"Doro is dead." I replied.

"Oh." Darkmarr uttered, somewhat crestfallen. "What happened?"

"We were on a job and things went sideways. He wanted me to tell you that he was sorry about what happened in Turin." I said.

"He said that?" Darkmarr asked.

"He did." I replied.

"Little Shit Bastard." Darkmarr's native Egyptian accent was starting to peek through the surface. "He has no right bringing up settled business."

"He was a time traveller, Prince. Whenever it happened was of no consequence. And clearly he felt some way about it. So I bring you the message. And this to me worthless hunk of obsidian" I concluded.

"It's pure darkness, Neil. To me, it is more precious than anything." Darkmarr stated. "I will grant you access to the vault in which the sigil lies. But your companion must stay with me. I don't get many visitors." Esmarelda and I looked at each other. "These are my terms." Darkmarr expounded.

"Fine" Esmarelda answered. "Got anything to drink?" She asked.

I left Esmarelda behind while I was led by guards to the vault. The vault was sealed, as I anticipated it would be. I waved a hand before it and dispelled the wards I had placed upon it. The vault door creaked open. Inside, on the floor of the vault, was the

Sigil of Loss.

Undoing this Sigil would not be so simple as the previous Sigils. I would have to make a sacrifice to undo this work. The sacrifice is never the choosing of the worker, but the choice of the sigil itself.

"I've come to tear you down" I spoke to the sigil

"Then you know my cost." The sigil of loss replied.

"Yes, you demand a sacrifice." I replied. "What is your demand?" I queried.

"A Hostess Twinkie" The sigil replied.

"A Hostess Twinkie?" I replied.

"Golden Snack Cake with Cream Filling." The sigil uttered. "That is my desire"

Puzzled, I reached into my satchel and pulled out a wrapped Hostess Twinkie ™ snack cake. "Here you are." I laid it on the sigil. The cake disappeared.

"I am satisfied," The sigil replied. "But when you return to your world you will find that item no longer exists." The sigil vanished in a glaze of green flame. I made my way back to the throne room as guided by the guard detail.

I returned to the Throne Room to find Esmarelda and the Prince of Shade locked in a rousing conversation. When I approached, the two of them conspicuously hushed.

"Oh, hey." Esmarelda called out to me.

"Have a good time?" I asked.

Esmeralda and Darkmarr looked at each other. A moment passed and laughter erupted between the two of them.

"Your friend here is delightful, Neil." Darkmarr said in a jovial tone.

"Are you laughing?" I asked.

"Well, um, yes" Darkmarr replied.

"I have never heard that." I said.

"Something has to come by that is worthy of laughter, Neil. You are incredibly boring." Darkmarr responded.

"I see." I replied, dejectedly.

"Neil. You never told me that you used to have a government job". Esmarelda chided.

"I was gone for like five minutes!" I called out exasperated. Esmarelda and Darkmarr laughed again at my annoyance. "I didn't work for the government, I worked with the government". Laughter erupted again. "I'm done here." I walked away.

"Okay, D. I'm gonna go tend to the party pooper. Catch you next time to get that Baklava recipe." Esmarelda spoke as she was leaving the Throne Room after me. Reaching me, Esmarelda pulled on my hand. "Such a spoilsport."

I pulled my hand away.

"Oh. so you're pouting now? Cool." Esmarelda said pointedly. "Let's get back to the mission then."

We floated back to the gossamer thread. I reached it and held onto it, giving it a tug to ensure it was still tied. I reached out my other hand to Esmarelda.

"Are you done with your tantrum?" She asked.

"Yeah. I just. I just gave up a lot back there and am feeling a little emotional." I spoke.

"What happened?" She asked, showing genuine concern.

"Earth doesn't have Twinkies any more"

Esmarelda looked at me in disbelief. We both erupted in laughter after a few seconds passed. "Okay." I said, finally catching my breath. "Let's get the fuck out of here"

"Sounds good." Esmeralda replied.   She threw herself around me and we ascended back into the Earth Dimension, sans Golden Caked goodness.

Part V

Sigil of Retribution

Esmarelda and I made our way back out of the casino without incident. I had never wanted a Twinkie more in my life. We got to the ride and sped off into the night.

"So, where to next?" Esmarelda inquired from the driver's seat, in some way implying she was steering the vehicle.

"This is the most dangerous and likely the most foolish part of our quest." I replied.

"That is an incredibly high bar, buddy." Esmeralda quipped.

"Do you want to know or not?" I spat.

"Of course I do, just trying to poke a little fun atcha." She replied.

"Ok. As I was saying. The fifth and final sigil is the sigil of retribution. And with a sigil like that there is a backlash. It's in the very nature of the thing." I expounded. "We need to locate the Archmage of Detroit. He is the guardian of the Sigil of Retribution." I concluded.

"I thought you were the Archmage." She replied.

"I was the Sorcerer Supreme. That is not the same as an Archmage. Archmages are tied to specific domains, and are not necessarily strictly involved in acting for the best interest of the place. An Archmage is not a protector so much as a landlord. They can be a good landlord or a shitty landlord as they see fit. But here's the rub. The Archmage draws power from their domain. The better the domain is doing and the more inhabitants believe in the Archmage, the more powerful the Archmage becomes. In our case, the Archmage has tricked the people of Detroit into believing he is an entrepreneur and real estate developer."

Esmarelda looked out at the night sky for a few minutes as we drove. We sat in silence until Esmarelda shattered it with an enthusiastic outburst. "Wait a minute." She said loudly and slowly. "Are we talking about...him?" She queried.

"Probably" I replied. "If you are asking about David Gill, then you would be absolutely correct. Meredith will be taking us to 1 Campus Martius. We will meet him in his office and we will explain our case." I stated.

"So we're just going to walk up there and what?" Esmarelda

asked.

"We are going to walk up there, go to his office and convince him to allow us to deactivate the Sigil" I answered.

"I have questions. Several, in fact" Esmarelda said. "One. How are we going to get inside? Two. Why would he be in his office in the middle of the night? Three. Why the fuck is he going to let us get at the sigil?" Esmarelda concluded.

"We are going to get inside by using our usual methods. Beguile and charm." I replied flatly..

Esmarelda rolled her eyes. "Ok so why would he even be there?" Esmarelda asked.

"Mr. Gill is always in his office. Even when he isn't in his office, he's in his office." I replied.

"What the fuck does that mean?" She asked.

"He is an adept of the magical arts. He is capable of splitting his consciousness and physical body into several forms. Any time you've seen him at a function or on television, heck even at his own meetings, that's just a golem that he is controlling remotely." I answered.

"Huh. That explains a thing or seven." She replied. "But

why would he help us?"

"We are going to explain how if he doesn't deactivate the sigil, there will be a massive karmic backlash that will likely come down his throat like a hot load of magma." I replied.

"Is that a bluff or is that legit?" Es asked.

"Well. These sigils have been holding a demonic entity. There were five of them. We've deactivated four of them. It's just a matter of time before the fifth fails. And when that happens…"

"The floor is lava." Esmeralda interrupted. "Got it."

"More or less." I confirmed.

"This is a plan. I like it. It's not a good plan, but it shows a lot of belief in your negotiation abilities. With someone who probably has more magical clout than you have these days. Sounds mint." Esmarelda grew quiet.

"I sense you have an issue with my strategy." I retorted.

"Yeah. I have an issue" She replied.

"So do you have a plan?" I asked.

"I have an idea. And sometimes ideas can be worth more than plans." She looked me straight in the eye. "Do you trust me, Neil?"

I started to answer, she cut me off.

"This isn't a bullshit trust conversation. Be very careful with the next words you use. Do. you. Trust. Me. Yes or no?" She maintained eye contact with me.

"I do," I answered.

"Then here's what we are going to do. I have been sharpening up on my doorways over the past couple of days. I've learned a couple of things." Esmarelda said with a grave tone.

"When?" I asked.

"When what?" She replied.

"When have you been studying gates?" I clarified.

"Last couple days, like I said." She replied with irritation. "Pay attention, Neil."

"I'm not trying to call you a liar, but I've been with you. I haven't seen you studying." I said pointedly.

"Magi aren't the only thing that can split their consciousness, Neil. That Hubris will get you killed if you don't get it under control" She said with a smirk.

I nodded with a cocked smile. "You're right." I said.

We drove toward downtown along Grand Avenue. It had

been so long since I had been to the city. From the other side of the country, all that you hear about is murder, corruption, and urban decay. No one talks about the lights of the Chrysler Building at night. The city really is a thing to behold. I guess a lot of that has to do with Gill. He has leveraged his magicks to bring more influence and wealth into the city. Not that he particularly cared about the people, but just as a means to an end. The better the city did, the better for him.

I never got to know him well enough to know what his motivations were. As a Necromancer, my interests were in spiritual energies and moving the Great Wheel. Gill is an Enchanter. He focuses his magickal energies on imbuing objects with spellcraft. A large number of his enchantments were structures, like buildings, stadiums, parks. His magic was visible everywhere in Detroit if you knew where to look.

But that's why Gill got involved with real estate as a cover. It allowed him access to places without question. And as the head of a corporation that was tending to these places, he could have undisturbed and unquestionable time to place his circles and enchantments. The properties managed by his company were in key locations in accordance with the placement of ley lines within the city. If you look at Detroit from overhead or even on a street map, you can see that the major streets fan out like a wheel. That is not some decision made by civil engineers. That is the influence of lines of power. Gill knew that as a Mage and used it to his advantage.

We pulled up to Campus Martius off of Woodward and Merdith pulled over to let us out. We exited the vehicle and she sped off. I gave her a little wave to keep the subterfuge of her being completely with a driver. Not that anyone would say shit. Detroit is a city of minding one's own fucking business. It's safer that way.

I motioned up to One Campus Martius, across the street from the Park. "This is it." I said to Esmarelda.

"Yep. That is certainly it." She replied. She was scanning the area, looking for something very specific.

"I don't think Starbucks is open," I joked.

"Fuck Starbucks. Last time I was down here, there were at least five places that could hand Starbucks their ass. But that's not what I'm looking for, silly man. I'm looking for a door, ``she said.

"Ah yes. Any chance I'll be able to see these at some point?" I asked.

"Not bloody likely. It's a fairy thing. You wouldn't get it." Esmarelda smirked.

"Sure." I assented. "I can defend the dimension from absolute annihilation, but I can't perceive fairy holes" I chuckled

"Don't fucking call them that!" She spun around with an outstretched index finger. I knew right away I had pushed things too far. I put my hands up apologetically.

"I got a little carried away in the moment." I said softly. "I meant no disrespect."

"Sure you did. And normally that's fine. But in this particular case it is very much not fine. Read the fucking room, Neil" Esmarelda walked away from me. I stood there, in my newfound admonishment. After walking thirty feet she stopped and stamped her feet. "Well." She said. "Are you coming or are you just going to mope a hole in the sidewalk?"

I hurried up to get alongside her. She looked up at me. She took hold of my cheek and jaw with her right hand. She looked deep into my eyes with a disarming glare.

"Now watch your fucking mouth with my people and show some respect." She gave me a little slap on the cheek.

Putting that behind us, we continued down Woodward with Esmarelda leading the way. She led me to the corner of Woodward and State. "This is it." She said. She pointed at a graffiti mural on a wall of an Eye of Osiris.

"Ah. Of course it is" I replied.

"You ready?" Esmeralda took my hand.

"Ready as I'm gonna be." I answered.

Hand in hand, we ran into and through the wall.

The city around us dissolved into a pure incandescent white light and absolute silence.

Part V section B: The Time Break

"Something went wrong." Esmarelda spoke in a small, almost childlike voice.

"We aren't supposed to be in what I can only describe as God's Waiting Room?" I asked

"Not the time, Dickhead." Esmeralda replied.

"So. Let's get back to basics," I said. "What were you trying to do?"

"I was opening a time door." She replied.

"A time door? Like time travel?" I asked.

"Yeah" Esmeralda snipped.

"I assume into the past?" I asked.

"Ish." Es said with indecision.

"I'm going to need something more than that," I said calmly.

"Well. You know how we can travel sideways in time?" Es asked.

"Yes. Like teleportation." I replied.

"Yeah like that. What I was attempting was like that but in a fuzzy way." She replied.

"A fuzzy way." I echoed

"I was trying to go inside Gill's office but like before you made the sigil." She replied.

"So we were going back in time and into an area obfuscated by powerful magicks." I crooked my mouth as I tried to run the equations in my head. "Yeah, that is probably a bit tricky."

"I can fix this," Esmarelda said with determination.

"I'm sure you can." I replied.

"I'm not sure I can." She confided. "I'm not exactly a scholar in time break studies"

"Time what now?" I asked.

"Time Break. It's when time travel is attempted, but instead ends up spawning an alternate pocket dimension. Something like we have here." She said with a building confidence.

"So can you unfuck it or not?" I asked.

"Well. The doors are tied to specific locations on Earth. Ley Line nexi." Esmarelda looked around. "I don't see anything like that."

"Well, we're alive. I can tell you that much." I replied. "I also can tell we are in a fixed location. We aren't moving, but we are still breathing which is weird. Even in the Astral Plane, the body does not interact with the environment as we are now."

"Can you use gateways?" She asked.

"Not any more. That left with the old gig." I answered.

"Balls!" Esmarelda exclaimed.

I looked around to get some sense of reasoning behind where or even what we were. White permeating light was emanating from everywhere and yet had no discernable source. The light was preventing the ability to see clearly any details around us, but was soft enough so that Esmarelda and I could still see each other well enough to interact.

"Wait. Shhh." I commanded. Esmarelda looked at me with a glare. "Do you hear something?"

We both stood silently, looking at each other. After a few seconds passed, Esmarelda opened her mouth to speak. I immediately held up a finger to hush her. About 1 minute after that, Esmarelda began to motion as if she were going to speak. I held the index finger out again but this time touching her lips, to accentuate the silent shush.

"If you don't get that finger off of me, I'm gonna bite it"

Esmarelda said very deliberately and oh so very quiet.

I heeded her warning and withdrew the errant digit. I held up the palm of my hand, which was found to be apparently more tolerable. In the distance, could be heard a light squeaking sound that could be none other than the slide of dry erase marker on a whiteboard. We looked away and once again established eye contact. Esmarelda's eyes widened. I nodded my head.

Once we could localize on the noise, we were able to lead our minds toward it. As the old saying goes, where the mind goes, energy flows. It appeared, based on our interaction with the environment around us, that we were in some kind of energy based universe. Esmarelda and I drifted closer to the light erratic squeaking until it bit by bit grew louder.

As we neared the source of the sound, the previously sterile white light had been replaced by gradual details of what appeared to be a study or what could only be described as a room that looks the way a small child thinks a smart person's office would look. There were several book cases, all filled with very important sounding books. Books with titles like "How to be the Best" and

"I'm Awesome, how are you?" and my personal favorite, "If you were me you wouldn't be in this mess". It was clear to me that I was looking at the self-help section of the bookcase. There were other books entitled, "Dragons", "Sweet Looking Swords", "King Stuff", "and one just entitled "Rad". This was clearly the history section.

In the center of the room was a desk with a conspicuously empty leather arm-chair. Esmarelda put her palm on the standing globe that was the height of her and gave it a hearty spin. We both stood and watched it spin with great satisfaction. Given the last segment of time, this was some welcome news. Fun can still be had, despite whatever the fuck this is that we are dealing with. We both stood and watched the globe spin until it slowed and eventually reached its termination. I felt a hand on my shoulder. It was decidedly not Esmarelda's hand.

I spun around to look as Esmarelda also put herself at the ready; the two of us almost knocking over the globe stand. Before us stood a slender gentleman, seemingly in his early twenties with long but well kempt brown hair and a pair of smart looking glasses. He was wearing a tweed suit vest and trousers with a jacket slung over his shoulder in his right hand.

"Can I help you folks?" He asked with an expectant grin.

"We sure as shit hope so! Esmarelda shouted.

"Now, dear. Tsk tsk. No need for profanity." The suited man countered.

"I apologize for my" I paused looking for some clue from Esmarelda as to what to call her. Seeing none, I continued, "associate's outburst." Esmarelda gave a half-hearted nod of approval. "We've had a very trying day and now seem to have gotten ourselves in a bit of a sticky situation." I explained.

"I'd say you've gotten yourself into a real pickle. A jam. A hot potato of a situation. A sticky widget." The suited man blathered on. "But where are my manners?" The man extended his hand to Esmarelda. She held her hand out flexing downward. "Enchante, mademoiselle." He spoke and kissed her outstretched hand. Esmarelda's cheeks seemed to redden ever so slightly. The suited man turned to me and put his hand out in the stereotyped overly enthusiastic handshake gesture. "Put 'er there, fella!" He commanded. I did indeed put 'er there. "I'm the Guy"

"The Guy?" I puzzled.

"Yeah. The Guy. If you'd rather you can call me Guy, or Mr. Guy." The Guy gave a wry half smile. "But rest assured, I am THE Guy." And with that the Guy winked at me.

"Are you like what, God then?" I asked. Completely disbelieving the words that were coming out of my mouth.

"No, I'm not God. Mainly because God is fake. I do match your limited human concept of what an Omnipotent, Omniscient, and Omnipresent being would be. So yes, Question Mark." The Guy replied.

Esmarelda and I stood gobsmacked before The Guy. He pulled a baseball from out of his vest pocket and started tossing it into the air and catching it. At first it was sporadic and then became more rhythmic. "I gotta tell ya. Usually people have questions for me. I'm not used to people jus getting here and not knowing what to do. It's like an entire cottage industry exists around my existence. And I tell ya, friendos, I am not disappointed with the adoration." The Guy caught the ball and placed it on a shelf. The Guy then sat down in his leather backed chair. "So, what can I do ya fer?"

"The Guy" I spoke while making air quotes, "I want you to

know something very specific about me. I have dealt with every type of being, entity and manifestation from any of the Outer Planes, Inner Planes, or Cross Dimensional Spaces. I had come pretty well to terms with the fact that there is no such thing as the One."

"This is known." The Guy replied.

"So why are you claiming to be just that?" I asked.

"I'm not." The Guy chuckled. "You have a limited understanding of the idea of limitlessness. When you made God, even in describing 'him' as infinite you gave 'him' definition." The Guy took a sip from a coffee mug with the logo for AC/DC. "It's all observer bias. The only thing humanity got right was the science, man! The science is hella rad!"

Esmarelda sat in one of the two newly appeared wooden chairs on the close side of the desk. "I'm gonna need a minute" She said, her voice dripping with defeat.

"It's okay sugar dumplin" The Guy condescended. He placed a hand to the side of his mouth as if to pantomime whispering "I'm doing a bit" The guy said to Esmarelda. Esmarelda's eyes lightened around the corners. "I reckon that little ol' me is gonna have to skeedaddle seeing on the count of not being possible an' all" Esmarelda chuckled at The Guy's comedic stylings.

"I like her." Esmarelda said.

"I kind of do too." I agreed. "Wait. You said her." I said.

"Yeah." Esmarelda said, waiting for me to say something else.

The Guy grinned at me. "Everyone brings something to the table. I'm not even real, remember? So back to the pickle."

"I tried to open a gateway in space and time and well, this happened." Esmarelda explained.

"Oh. You broke time. Just that?." The Guy said dismissively.

"That sounds pretty serious." I interjected.

"It can be." The Guy explained. "But seeing as time is a construct, meh. Not always"

"So, how do we get back?" I asked.

The Guy let out a chuckle. "Oh. That can't happen. You broke time, you fool! What were you planning to go back to, an infinite loop of matter creating and destroying itself, because spoiler alert that's what you got."

"That's shitty." Esmarelda said.

"It's whatever." The Guy said. "You can move on to a new place. One with a better vibe"

"Are you serious, right now?" I asked.

"Not in the least." The Guy replied. "I am a lottle concerned that you would think you can intimidate what was just explained as an infinitely powerful being. Lottle by the way is a word I just made up as a portmanteau of Lot and Little. It's ironic. Like your existence." The Guy stared at me quite unamused. "Now how about you stop being a petulant child and tell me what you were trying to do when you broke the fundamental laws of reality"

Esmarelda chimed in. "We were working on a mission to save the world."

"Pointless, but go on." The Guy replied.

We both felt like our dog got run over in front of us.

"What do you mean, pointless?" I asked.

"This one's a lock. The world is ending. It's just that time hasn't caught up. You remember time, that thing you broke." The Guy flipped his hair over at Esmeralda. "So this demon you've been trying to release so you can send it to its home. Do you remember why you were trying to do that?"

"Unfinished business" I replied

"Wrong!" The Guy yelled. "Wrong, wrong, wrong, wrong, wrong! You are a pawn. The (consults notes) Dark Star wants to be free so it can make it's way back to it's home world to enact revenge. When you free it, that's all it's gonna do, baby."

"And it will happen now either way because four of the five sigils are deactivated" I muttered.

"Pre-cisely" The Guy exclaimed. "So, why not explore some other options?"

"What do you mean, other options?" I asked.

"You can't win this scenario, Necrodaddy." The Guy said with a wink.

"Ok." I said

"What do you mean o-k?" The Guy asked.

"My friend and I need safe passage back to our home dimension. And you have to give it to us. There are rules. And now that I know what this is, you have to follow them." I said with authority.

Esmarelda turned toward me, "What's going on here?" she asked.

"Yeah, Neil. What exactly IS going on here?" The Guy mocked.

"We are done here." I replied. "That is what is going on. I'm done with your tricks. I don't know why I didn't see it before but I do now. I thought you were dead. I should have known better."

"Okay. I guess the subterfuge has outlived its usefulness." The Guy said with a crestfallen tone.

"So, Jonny. What's it gonna be? Are you going to send us back or am I gonna have to pull out the Hammer?" I asked. "This can be nice or I can get not nice."

"You think you can just push me around?" Jonny popped off.

"You're a spirit, Doro. I can do whatever. The fuck. I want." With my final utterance, I pulled the festering sore on the face of the timestream that was Jonny D'oro into an amethyst. He pulled with everything he had but I still prevailed. He was not dead but he was still a spirit. And being a spirit he was firmly in my domain. When Doro was finished being pulled into the gem, we found ourselves back at State and Woodward, right where we left off.

I shoved the amethyst in my pocket. "And I'll deal with you later." I said to the gemstone.

I turned to Esmarelda and pointed at her. "Okay. Let's not do that again."

Esmarelda chuckled "You got a deal, Neil." She chuckled again, "Heh that rhymed."

I looked wordlessly at Esmeralda.

"C'mon. It's funny." She said in a tone of feigned indignance. "Fine, suit yourself." She walked a few steps away and said just loudly enough for me to hear, "square" She turned back and flashed me a wry smile. "So what's next, stud?"

I flipped the amethyst into the air and caught it. "We see a man about a sigil"

"You got a deal…" Esmarelda stopped herself and chuckled before she made the same joke again. She shoved against me and slipped her arm around mine. She squeezed my arm tightly and we made our way back toward One Campus Martius.

"So, Neal. What's the story with the guy?" Esmarelda asked.

"Which guy"?" I asked.

"You have an incredibly short attention span, my sweet." Esmarelda replied. "The Guy in the gemstone in your pocket"

"Oh, that piece of shit." I answered. "That's none other than Mr. Jonny D'oro"

"I got that much." Esmarelda said jokingly, "I mean clearly you two have a past. Give up the deets, man."

"There's a lot there. How much do you want to know?" I asked.

"I think as much information as you can give me is beneficial. That way I can make informed decisions about what I am getting myself into." She clarified.

"Don't you think that you are already in?" I asked.

"If you have to ask the question.." She trailed off with a chuckle.

I stopped in front of the Braziliian steakhouse. "I'm serious here, Esmarelda. You are already in for the duration."

"I can walk away any time I choose, Neil. Don't get me fucked up. I'm here because I choose it. I choose you." Esmarelda started walking again without me.

"Ok" I answered.

She stopped, keeping herself turned away from me. A few minutes passed. "Ok, what?"

"Ok, I'll give you the story, but it's not a short one" I explained.

"We have a few minutes." She said with a smirk.

"Where to start. Topeka, Kansas, 1935" I replied.

"We should get some coffee. I know a place that is open." Esmarelda took my hand and she led me to a coffee shop a block away.

Part 5 section C: Jonny, the Topeka Five and Exactly How Much Pressure It Takes To Break a Diamond

We arrived at the cafe. It had a sign out front that read "Joe's Cafe". It had a charm and sensibility that came from a bygone era that perhaps never was. We entered the cafe and were greeted by a waitress. Her name tag read "Flo". The waitress led us to a table in a corner opposite two old men who were reading newspapers, drinking black coffee, smoking hand rolled cigarettes. When we walked by, one of the men reached out and motioned to us, saying something in a dialect of Arabic that I did not recognize. Esmarelda said something back to them with a polite smile and walked to the man. He handed her a cigarette and lit it for her. She thanked him, I understood that much. She walked back to me, the lit cigarette still in her mouth.

She had a smile on her lips. "What was that about?" I asked.

"He wanted to know if I wanted a cigarette. I didn't want to let him down, so I obliged." Esmarelda replied. "Wouldn't want to be rude, after all."

"You are a picture of manners, my dear." I said flatly.

We sat at the table designated for us.

"You two want coffee?" Flo asked.

"I do." I answered

"Same" Esmarelda added.

"Excuse me, miss." I asked Flo as she turned to walk away.

"Yeah?" She chirped.

"Is it ok to smoke in here?" I asked.

"We exist beyond the confinement of social contract." Flo said in a thick Iranian accent. "Feel free." Flo walked away into the back, presumably to get our coffees. I could not be too sure with that answer.

"This is a good fucking cigarette." Esmarelda told me.

"I bet. Hand rolled usually are." I replied.

"Want a drag?" She asked.

"Not thanks. I have to be in a certain head space and…"

"Suit yourself." She cut me off. She took a long cool drag and looked out the window at the street.

"So, you wanna know the whole deal. Here's the whole deal." I opened sternly. "In 1935, the Government started fucking around with a substance called Dead Star Matter. It's basically a little glob of universal jelly that exists after the collapse of a star. They called it DSM. The Germans figured out how to syphon DSM from collapsing stars through wormhole technology. That's the real reason the Americans got involved in the War, to stop Germany from building an army of superhumans. It had fuckall to do with the Holocaust" I stopped. "I think I would like a hit, if the offer still stands."

Esmarelda stood up abruptly. "I got you one better." She walked to the old men and returned with another cigarette and a single stick match. "Here you go. Amir sends his regards."

"What did you tell them?" I asked with amazement.

"I told them my old man is an asshole and left the house without cigarettes." She laughed. I knew she wasn't kidding. I took the hand roll and lit it with the stick match. I waved at the old men. They waved back amiably. I took a deep, acrid hit. The tobacco was a special blend. One I haven't had in many years. It was welcome in my lungs, but I still coughed. 'Easy there, killer" Esmarelda put her hand on my back. "You'll ruin my rep as a bad kid" She laughed with a twinkle in her eye.

"So. The United States, not to be outdone by the Nazis, developed their own super soldier program. It was called, Project: Delphi." I laid down my cigarette on a saucer to sip my turkish coffee. "There were six superhumans that were created in a lab in Topeka Kansas on March 23rd, 1935. One of them was the bastard you just met, the four others were Mantis, John Solomon, Darkmarr, Natasha, and a gentleman named Tabernacle. You've met Mantis, Darkmarr and Natasha of course. You won't meet Solomon. You should hope you never meet Tabernacle." I took another drag. My lungs were now attenuated to the smoke.

"Long story short, they flew to Berlin and kicked the shit out of Fuhrer?" Esmarelda asked.

"More or less." I answered. The story is less about what happened in the war and more about what happened after the war. After the war, Doro had his memory wiped. He started to get it back in 1975, when he started working for The Resistance here in Detroit. Which is where I met up with him in early 2000's. I ran with the crew for a while and well, things went south."

"What makes him such a bastard? I mean it seems like you have a pretty high tolerance for fuckery." Esmarelda sipped from her cup.

"Jonny is a racist, misogynist, and used his powers for evil."
I answered.

"Oh. So like a super criminal or something?" She asked.

"He would use his mastery of time to seduce women.
Basically form a time loop where he would meet them a dozen
times and use everything he learned to make it appear he was their
soulmate." I said.

"That's a stupid way to use time control powers. Why
wouldn't he just, I dunno, use it to become fabulously rich or
something?" She asked.

"Because he got off on making his conquests do things that
they would not normally be inclined to do. And I'll just leave it at
that." I looked out the window.

"So he was low key rapey is what you're saying?"
Esmarelda asked.

"Yep." I answered.

"Lot of guys running around like that." Esmarelda took a
drag and stared off. "How do you decide which ones need killin' on
that criteria?"

"Wasn't just that." I replied. "It sets the stage. With his powers increasing over time, he needed progressive thrills to get his kicks. So eventually he would seduce entire family lines of women. And then, when he started extending out into different timelines and realities...he became a problem. He stopped caring if he was creating paradoxes any more."

"Oh" Esmarelda was hit with the weight of what she heard.

"Yeah." I confirmed. "So I was sent to find him. A couple years ago, he was my Halloween surprise. So I did what I had to do."

"You killed him?" Esmarelda asked.

"Not quite." I answered. "I tricked him into becoming a Djinn"

"That sounds like a terrible idea for someone who has a serious problem with narcissism. Give them near infinite powers. How did that work out for you?" She asked.

"He was stuck in a pocket dimension." I replied

"The one we just popped into." Esmarelda said.

"Yep" I replied. "So Djinn, being spirits, are something I am quite handy with. I just didn't know it was him. Had I known where we were I would've cleaned his clock."

"You seem like you are still holding a grudge, Neil." Esmarelda pointed out.

"I just don't like it when people use their strength to hurt weaker people. We have a responsibility." I said.

"You have a responsibility. I have a tiny bladder. See you in a bit" She got up to excuse herself to the restroom. In her absence, I sipped my coffee and smoked what was left of my cigarette. Esmarelda came back wearing a uniform from the security company that tends to One Campus Martius.

"And where did you manage to find that?" I asked with a laugh.

"I just find things. Don't you know that by now, Neil." Esmarelda stroked the side of my face. "Okay let's go talk to a man about a sigil"

We walked the rest of the way to One Campus Martius. I made myself invisible and Esmarelda entered without issue. We moved effortlessly to the sixth floor, where Gil's office was. When we got close enough, I reached out through the astral plane to contact him.

"Archmage of Detroit, I have an offer for you." I projected.

"Hawthorn? I thought I quit maging" Gil replied.

"I have a few more things to work out. I need your help. And I have a token" I replied.

"Come on up." He said.

I directed Esmarelda to David Gil's office. We made our way in without any security issues. We were expected, after all. Gil's office was everything I imagined it would be. Sparse, utilitarian, and full of hidden geomancy. Sigils everywhere. Mundanes couldn't read them but they lit up like Christmas to those that knew what they were seeing.

"Neil" David addressed us from his chair. "You brought a friend." He smiled.

"This is Esmarelda. She is...my bodyguard." I answered.

"I'm sure she is." Gil answered with a smug chuckle. The Archmage rose and leaned on an ornate cane. Gil took a few beleaguered steps toward the two of us.

"What's up with the cane?" Esmarelda asked bluntly.

"She's direct, isn't she?" Gil asked me.

"Indeed. It's part of her charm." I smirked.

Esmarelda took off her uniform cap, letting her hair spill down the left side of her face. Gil narrowed his eyes. "I remember you." He said.

"Yeah. We've met." Esmarelda answered without explanation.

"I had a stroke a few months back. Really took the wind out of me." Gil answered.

"That's unfortunate." I answered.

"Yeah. That's why I didn't take your job. A lesser man would have died." Gil bragged.

"A lesser man wouldn't have gotten into that trouble" I countered.

"Fair enough" He replied. "Gotta eat your own dog food"

Esmarelda rolled her eyes and sighed. I knew better than to ask,

"I have a proposition for you, Mr. Gil." I said, breaking the tension. "I need to take down the Sigil of Retribution"

Everyone stood silently for about a minute.

"That's incredibly foolish, Hawthorne." Gil said. "Why would you want to do a silly thing like that?"

"The Dark Star was not properly dealt with. I need to release it so I can destroy it." I replied.

"I'm afraid I can't allow that." Gil replied.

"I can see we've gone past negotiations," I said. "The other four sigils have been taken down already." David's face went blank at my revelation. "But. I have compensation for your help." I pulled the amethyst out of my pocket.

Gil sniffed the air. "Is that who I think it is?"

"Indeed. The little bastard himself." I confirmed.

Gil motioned for us to back up. Esmarelda and I complied. In the center of the room lay an ornate rug. Gil rolled a corner of it up to reveal the Sigil of Retribution. "Here you go, folks." He said. Esmarelda and I looked at each other nervously. I drew in a deep breath.

"You should leave," I said to The Archmage.

"That's not going to happen, Hawthorne," He replied.

"Ok. It's about to get sticky in here." I warned.

I moved my hands in the air to dispel the Sigil. The room

started shaking. The lights went out and the emergency generator kicked in. When the lights came back on, the room was filled with circling, viscous black ooze.

Esmarelda, David, and myself off uttered in unison a resounding "Shit"

Chapter 12: The Dark Star Rises

As the swirling mass of cohesive darkness formed a vortex around us, I felt a much deserved sense of impending doom.

"I get the sense that this is not how you envisioned this going, Hawthorne" Gil chimed in.

"No, David, this is not how I envisioned this going." I replied.

"Any ideas?" Gil asked.

The whirl of black goo spun around us in several distinct cycles.

"You did say it was going to get sticky." Esmarelda quipped.

"I hardly think this is the time for jokes," I fired back.

"I like her," Gil commented.

"Oh yeah, why did you let that asshole fire me then?" She jabbed.

"What?" Gil replied.

"Nothing," Es said. "Let's get out of here"

"Not sure how we're gonna do that." I replied. "Any exit we have would lead us right through that shit. I'm sure between the three of us we…"

"Now I KNOW you are not talking about containing this thing, Neil!" Esmarelda screamed at me.

"Kinda." I said sheepishly.

"Gah! Didn't we just the fuck get gahhh fuck just fuck." Esmarelda devolved into incoherent cursing.

"What do we know about it?" Gil asked.

"We know it likes to possess children and generally fuck up days." I replied.

"No children here" Gil replied.

"Nope no children here" Esmarelda added.

The building started to tremble as the energy of the Dark Star began to build in the vortex.

"Es. Can you gate us out?" I asked.

"Maybe." Esmarelda replied. "Just based on last time, I have a heckin concern"

"What happened last time?" Gil asked.

"Don't worry about it." Esmarelda replied above the

cacophonous groan of the building starting to rend asunder beneath the weight of the tumult.

"We are going to die here if we don't" I yelled in desperation.

"Ugh. Fine." Esmarelda opened a gate. "C'mon"

I jumped through. Esmarelda leapt after me, throwing the Detroit Salute at Gil as the building toppled around him. We popped out at Campus Martius Park. I looked around.

"Where's Gil?" I asked Esmarelda.

"It's not about who is right, it's about what is right" She replied.

I looked at her. "You left him to die, didn't you?" I asked.

"Innovation is rewarded. Execution is worshipped" She replied.

"I'm sure he'll be fine. Archmage and all. But about that?" I extended my arm and pointed at the vortex leading out of what was One Campus Martius into the night sky. "Gonna be hard to explain that one away."

"That's a lot to unpack." Esmarelda said.

We both stood in silent terror at the growing whirlwind of dark energies.

"It's getting bigger Neil. What should we do?" Esmarelda asked.

"Running is out of the question at this point." I answered.

"Do you hear that?" Esmarelda asked.

A faint whistle could be heard in the distance. Initially it could only barely be heard above the chaos of the Dark Star. But as the seconds drew on, it became louder and more rhythmic. A chug of steam overlaid above a piercing keening cry akin to a banshee. "Is that…?" I started to ask a completely unnecessary question.

The night sky was cut in half by a streak of a spectral locomotive piercing across the Detroit Skyline from out of the River slamming squarely into the swirling mass that is the dark star. Green Smoke and neon green flames rose out from the impact site. The train passed through and circled back through the air, getting more water from the river and coming back to pummel into the slimenado.

"Holy Shit. It's the God Damn Ghost Train!" I exclaimed.

"Fuck yeah, Ghost Train!" Esmarelda added.

The two of us high fived, maintaining eye contact

aggressively.

The Ghost Train made several passes and the Dark Star, blowing blazing neon green holes in the undulating mass with every trip. After half a dozen runs, the Dark Star disappeared, and the Ghost Train reached a rest at Campus Martius Park. Esmarelda and I stood before the Ghost Train, billows of green smoke issuing from beneath the spectral chassis. The Engineer climbed out of the Engine. He floated down to solid ground and tipped his cap.

His ghostly wisp of a handlebar mustache waved in a non-existent wind. He pulled a pocket watch out of his vest and viewed it with alarm. "You've made me get off schedule." The Engineer groaned. "I'm gonna need some kind of compensation to bring back to make this allright." He demanded.

I started to balk, then I looked down at my boot. The amethyst that held Jonny Doro was resting squarely on my toe cup. It must have blown clear of One Campus Martius when it finally collapsed. I pointed down at the gem. "What about that?"

The engineer eyed the gem and looked back at me with a toothless grin across his face. "Son, you've got yourself a deal" The Engineer jutted an ectoplasmic tendril down to my foot and licked up the amethyst, leaving a green slime trail behind. The Engineer floated back atop the Ghost Train and took off back into the Detroit River.

"Ok. That was fucking rad." I said to Esmarelda.

"You have no idea how long I have waited for that to happen, Neil" She replied.

"We have more work to do though" I said with a sigh.

"Clean up around here?" She asked.

"Shhh. No." I chuckled. "This will be sorted before sunrise. The city takes care of herself. We have to get back to Brighton to finish off the Dark Star." I said.

"You mean it isn't dead?" Esmarelda posited

"No. Just the Messenger. The real deal is back at the house on Fairlane" I confessed.

"Fair enough. You ready for a hop?" Esmarelda said with a wink. She opened a portal gate on the side of a building.

"See, when you're winking like that I feel like there is some double meaning" I said with a chuckle.

"Get your mind out of the gutter, Neil. Let's go bust some

space demon ass wide open." Esmarelda said, this time winking with both eyes in tandem.

"Cool." I replied.

We jumped into the doorway and journeyed back to my ancestral home.

Chapter 13: The Final Chapter

This is it, I thought. I walked through the doorway that
Esmarelda had created. She stood on the other side ushering me
through. When I passed through, she closed it. We stood in my
parent's drive-way. Right about the spot that my brother and I used
to shoot hoops. The basketball hoop was no longer there, but
some vestigial semblance of my memories still remained. I didn't
have too many good ones, but somehow they peeked out every so
often.

I stood transfixed. Esmarelda gave me a quick nudge to
knock me out of my trance.

"You okay there, Chief." She asked.

"Okay as I'm going to be, I guess." I answered. "It knows
that we are here to kill it."

"It can know it all night, not gonna change shit about it."
Esmarelda commented.

"True enough." I said. I rubbed the lucky rabbit's foot I held
in my pocket right next to my Grandad's Pocket Watch and my
Buffalo Nickel. I had all the trappings that I needed to do battle the

way I needed to. Esmarelda reached out and took me hand. She felt warmer than she had ever felt before. Maybe it was just the crisp of the autumn air or maybe that all my blood had settled into my feet, but something about the energy moving through our hands made me not want to break that moment. Maybe if I played my cards right we could stay in it forever.

"So." She said gently. "Have you found your balls yet or do you need me to send in a search party?"

There it was. No need for sentimentality when there was work to do. I took my hand out of my pocket and put a hand on either side of my face. "You, my dear, are a true treasure."

"You say that like you're intending to bury me somewhere and leave a pirate map." She smirked.

"The night's still young." I quipped.

Esmarelda slugged me on the arm and walked to the house. We entered through the open garage. All the trappings of my father's former life were present. I hadn't noticed them before but I was operating on tunnel vision. All of the yard implements. Some old junk that I was never able to properly identify. A couple of bamboo fishing rods that we never fished with. And a twenty five pound compound bows. Esmarelda spotted the bow the same time I did.

"Ooh. Got any arrows for this thing?" She asked with excitement.

"Like I've been here in twenty years, Ez." I replied.

'Fair enough." She reached a hand into the maelstrom. "Here we go." She reached out with a full quiver of arrows. I am nearly certain that wasn't there before. I am beyond surprise any more. She wills it and it happens. One of her many charms. I put my hand on the oor into the house.

I felt a chill run through the door handle. A near electric flow. I let go of the doorknob.

"Wards" I said to Es.

"Fuck that. This is your place as much as anyone else's. Cut 'em down." Es commanded.

I heeded her word and took down the ward with a flick of my wrist and opened the door. We crossed the threshold. Es drew the bow and knocked an arrow.

"Really?" I looked at her and asked.

"Oh yeah. It's like that." She replied.

"Fuck me. When else are you gonna get to snipe moon ghosts with a piece of shit bow.?" I jestd.

"There is much truth in your words Neil." Es replied.

"there always is." I replied. "There's the basement," I pointed.

"I'm gonna let you lead for a change." Es said.

I opened the basement door. A massive ball of hair and fury, all claws and fangs leapt upon me from the stairwell. I knew this was an illusion that was placed by the Shadow King. I went into my mind palace to dispel the illusion, closing my eyes and breathing deeply.

"What the bloody fuckballs are you doing Neil?" Esmarelda screamed. The beast took a chunk of my shoulder with its teeth. I had clearly made a miscalculation. Esmarelda zipped two arrows into the eyes of the Thing. The creature's head immediately burst into flame and the thing was rendered to ash. She leaned down and spoke some words in an unknown tongue and touched the wound, causing them to close up except for a wicked scar. "Sorry I couldn't heal the whole thing" She whispered. Resuming a normal, conversant tone, "That was a goddamn werewolf, Neil. I know I don't need to tell you that. Get your game face on. I can't keep saving your ass." She walked ahead muttering "Dirty fucking casual"

Cresting the bottom of the stairs, I stood up to join her. "Fuck get your ass down here!" She yelled. I ran down the stairs. The entirety of the basement had been consumed by a massive, tentacled horror. Esmarelda, never losing sight of the monstrosity, Spoke to me. "That is not a fucking shadow, neil. I don't feel like you conducted your research."

"No, my dear. That's the Dark Star. It's reached its final form." I said in a monotone

"Riiight." She said in a broken mock cockney. "Plan then?"

"We walk back up the stairs slowly and carefully." I said very quietly. There wouldn't be time for that. A tentacle shot out and wrapped around my ankle. It ripped me into the air and held me there.

"Ok." Esmarelda said to herself. "I guess I am spending the whole night getting you out of trouble."

The tendrils of black goo enveloped me and infiltrated my mouth. I helplessly stayed dangling in the air, struggling against the insurmountable strength of the denizen of the darkness. The last thing I remember before succumbing to unconsciousness was the warrior scream of Esmarelda, like a war hardened Valkyrie claiming the dead for Valhalla, charging toward me and the fiend.

I awoke on the back deck. My shirt was torn off and I had burns all over. Esmarelda stood over me, turned away, as if guarding me from some unseen force. I had the bitter, metallic taste in my mouth, as if I had been binging on Vegemite. I guess it shouldn't surprise me that the taste of ultimate indelible evil should be identical to the taste of one of Australia's largest commercial food exports.

I had flashes in my memory of Nyx's respirator masked face and the shadow of mechanical bellows working furiously in front of a massive coal fire. It wasn't imagined, but a place I had really been. The memory was implanted in the house of terror and foreboding. As if it were simultaneously a recollection and an internal warning against a thing that should not be. The end of the memory was the mechanical whisper of "That ought do." by Doctor Nyx. I felt a stinging like a post hole digger tearing through my chest. With that trauma I was snapped back into the present.

Esmarelda heaving like a terrifying monster in her own right, still ever vigilant.

"Narf." I muttered.

""Good, you're awake. Let's get the hell out of here." She commanded. "On your feet"

I reached down and touched my chest. My eyes were sprung open with the horror of my discovery. It appeared as if half of my chest had been replaced with mechanical parts.

"What....what happened to me?" I felt myself start to sicken.

"That crazy technolich came and bandaged you up. The goo got a hold of you. I cut you out and got you up the stairs, but it had worked its way into your heart. Before I knew what had happened, It was here taking you to some pocket dimension and doing surgery on you."

"Well, that's a lot to unpack." I replied, my breath labored.

"Well, let's start with you're not dead and the Dark Star is not inside you." Es consoled.

"The death I can handle. The possession is unacceptable." I made a lame attempt at a joke.

"But we really do need to get moving. Between that thing

and the Moon Ghosts, this is not an ideal spot for a last stand." Es said.

"The Moon Ghosts showed?" I asked.

"Not yet, but I feel like it's a forgone conclusion at this point". She replied. Es got me to my feet and I ambled weakly. "That's the spirit."

"We're in for a treat now." I looked to the sky above the backyard. The swirling vortex of star matter started to appear again, in much the same way it did earlier and likely to a lesser extend the way it did when I was a babe. Esmarelda supported me as we hobbled to the Cadillac. One steep after the other, slowly and surely. We had to pass by the vortex to get to the driveway. She fearlessly clutched onto me and spirited me past the nonsense. We got to the car. She let go of me for the briefest of moments to open the car door.

I was swept up in the vortex. As I became part of the maelstrom, her screams were the last connection I had with the reality of that world. I was held in midair. It was as if I was being drawn apart by invisible forces. My arms were outstretched as well as my legs. I felt the internal integrity of my limb joints starting to crack and tear beneath the force of what was rending me asunder.

I felt a low rumble start to amass from the ground tens of feet below me. It started like thunder but slowly became more focal. Then I could hear patterns of sound resounding into words. This was no mere mortal phenomenon. The power that was attempting to draw me into the sky and ultimately tear me apart had angered some great spirit that dwelled in this land. I don't believe in salvation, at least not the way most folks refer to it, but this was coming pretty close.

I heard a voice booming from beyond the landscape and within all things. It started to overcome the roar of the vortex, which was no longer just a vortex. A few hundred feet above me there was a flurry of lights in an elliptical shape. I was being drawn toward the ellipse. As I drew closer to the shape, I could better make out that it was no mere egg shaped ball of light, but what could only be described as a flying saucer.

In all my years and all of my experiences, I have never seen an actual real deal unidentified flying object before. I've dealt with creatures living under the oceans that act like what the normals feel to be aliens. I've dealt with extra-dimensional entities. I've crossed paths of demons, angels, and gods. But I have never had any dealings with any motherfucking u.f.o. As they say, there is a first time for everything.

There I was, a couple hundred feet in the air. I could see this was my untimely end. I chuckled a little, thinking of all the close scrapes I have had with all manner of mystical and mythical beast. And this, some fucking aliens that probably had giant cantalope shaped heads and eyes like alt rock guitarists. I'm sure that reference was for no one but me and the four other folks that remember Limp Bizkit, but anyway.

As I drew closer, I felt a peace flow over me. An acceptance that I was unable to affect any change. For all my knowledge and experiences, this piece of shit was going to end me with some ridiculous death ray. In the clarity, it occurred to me that I still didn't know exactly what I was dealing with. And what about me was so damn interesting to these extraterrestrials?

I heard the words start again, this time with more intensity. I remembered that Esmarelda was standing on the ground, helplessly watching me pulled into a ship for some kind of interstellar abduction. Two things I've learned about that lady throughout our time together, number one she is never helpless and two she doesn't process emotion like a human. What I imagine to be her experience at seeing me swept away is probably nowhere even close to what she was actually going through. The words I was hearing from outside my invisible prison were not her after all. I know that voice.

"Now you put that boy down, right now!" I heard a woman yell,

Oh shit. That was Grammy. These aliens done fucked up.

"Maybe you didn't hear me." I heard in her raspy Kentucky drawl. "I said put my grandson down and get your asses back to wherever you come from. I ain't mad about you being from far away, but you need to leave my Neil alone."

The space craft started moving it's way toward the ground with me in tow. I was released to the ground. Grammy continued to address the ship.

"Now come on out and sit a spell." She said. The ship was

now resting on the ground. It was an egg shaped semi-sphere that was perfectly shined and did not appear to have any openings. "I don't think you boys heard me." Knowing her as well as I had, I could tell she was getting annoyed. It was not wise to annoy Grammy, even when she was alive and a mere mortal. Now with the powers of the grave at her disposal, no way no how. One hundred percent would not fuck with. The lights issuing from the craft had settled down and there were no longer any errant winds.

"Alright now." She called. "Don't be shy. Show me your face."

Esmarelda ran to me to assess my situation. "Are you doing okay?" She asked.

"I've had a very eventful few minutes here. I was possessed by Space Demon, Had a mechanical heart transplant, nearly abducted into what I presume to be space, and..."

"I get it. You can shut up now." Esmarelda interrupted.

Grammy spoke again, this time with more authority. "Now get your asses out here and talk to an old woman."

The craft opened an aperture. First it was a pinpoint then expanded into a hole the size of a human. As the metamorphosis progressed, the craft was transformed into a hollow semi-lunar formation. Two spindly armed and legged grey humanoids with giant heads and enormous black shiny eyes walked toward Grammy. Just like I fucking thought.

"Now what do you boys intend to do here?" Grammy asked.

The Greys communicated using thoughts instead of words. "We have been following your Grandson for many years. He has secrets lying within his genetic code. We were intending to bring him back to our homeworld and use that code as a means of ending the Blood-Space War."

"That sounds like it may hurt my little boy" Grammy spoke using her words.

"It would involve him being disassembled as an organic entity and live on forever as a martyr to our cause." The Greys responded telepathically

"Now I don't reckon that is something that is none too pleasant, and I don't reckon that my Neil would want any part of that." Grammy replied again in speech. She turned her attention to me. "Neil, Sweetie, would you want to be torn apart and become a space weapon?" Grammy asked.

"Can't say that I would Grammy." I answered

"Well there you go. You fellers can get back in your boat and get on back home without my special boy." Grammy gave the Greys their marching orders.

"That is not acceptable. Without his Power, we will be eradicated as a species. Without him we will face extinction." The Greys rebutted.

"If you don't get back in that thing and high tail it out of here, it won't matter none to you." Grammy inflected.

The Greys looked at each other. Then looked at me. Then looked at each other. Then back to Grammy. One of them held a hand up and addressed Grammy. '

"We apologize for the harm we have caused your family. You will not hear from us again." The Greys announced. They walked back into their ship, sealed it up and jettisoned into the night sky. In seconds, they were gone.

"Now that's it for that." Grammy said to me. "Who's this beautiful creature?" She asked motioning to Esmarelda.

"That's my....that's" I stuttered.

"My name is [REDACTED]." Esmarelda said to Grammy. As

soon as I heard the name, it slithered out of my mind like a mischievous garter snake. "It's a pleasure to make your acquaintance." She curtsied.

Grammy turned back to me. "I'm glad to see you finally have a sweet girl to take care of you. Now I can be at rest." Grammy started to fade away. "I don't have to worry about you anymore. But before I go, I have one more thing to say."

'What's that Grammy?" I asked, getting to my feet.

"You need to burn that house down. Damn thing is full of ghosts" She continued dissipating into the scenery, laughing her restricted high pitched cackle like only a hill-folk witch like herself could. I never put together that she was a witch while she was alive, but it's so apparent now. It's like I can't imagine a time I felt otherwise. She was not a person to be taken lightly.

"I reckon we got us a house to burn" I said to Esmarelda.

"I'm game," She said.

We approached the house, hand in hand. "How are we gonna do this?" I asked.

Esmarelda pulled out the largest piece of hematite I have ever seen in my life from apparently nowhere. "This"

"What are we going to do, aggressively cleanse their chakras?" I quipped.

"No, fucker. Hematite is flammable. Everyone knows that. Duh" Esmarelda chastised.

"How could I forget?" I laughed.

Esmarelda with her Hematite Boulder and I with my Grandad's Watch stepped toward the House of Long Shadows. A pillar of light appeared from the garage in front of us.

"For fuck's sake! What now?!?" I yelled.

A woman with long auburn hair and wispy pink tulle gown stepped out of the column. She was heavily backlit and I could only really make out her after-image.

"Oh shit." Esmarelda said to herself quietly. If fae crossed themselves, I think she would've. She dropped to a knee before the woman.

"Rise, my child." The mysterious woman bade Esmarelda.

Esmarelda rose to her feet and kissed the woman's hand.

The light receded and I got a better look at the mystery woman.

I found myself speaking before I was able to censor myself.

"Holy Fuck? Is that Kate Bush?"

"Fool!" Esmarelda admonished me. "That is Mab, Queen of the Fae."

"I'm confused. You look just like Kate from the cover of the Hounds of Love LP." I explained myself as best I could.

"You see me as you wish to see me" Queen Mab explained. "Humans are incapable of seeing our kind. They can only see their impression of our kind."

"So why do you look like Kate Bush then?" I asked quizzically.

"Because that is your elemental expression of regality" She stated matter of factly.

I looked at Esmeralda and things started to click into place.

"Child." Titania said to Esmarelda. "It's time to come home. You've had enough fun with this mortal." Titania turned back to me. "Thank you for all you've done. The Court owes you a debt of gratitude and honor." She kissed my forehead. "The Sidhe always repay their debts"

Returning her attention to Esmarelda. "Come now, Child". Titania turned and walked away into a newly opened doorway.

Esmarelda turned to me and took a step closer. "I have to go away now." She said quietly, as if not to make it not real. I could see tears forming in the corners of her eyes. "Remember when I'm gone. Remember I was here. And with you." A tear trickled down her cheek. "Will you do that for me?"

I wiped a tear from her cheek. It turned into an onyx shard in my hand. "You'll always be a part of me." I promised. She kissed me, and then vanished into the doorway. On the way through she whispered something but I didn't make it out.

I was alone in the garage. I looked to my feet and saw that giant fucking hematite.

"Duh." I said to myself.

I hefted the hematite on my shoulder and kicked in the door.

Chapter 14: The Road Less Traveled

I met Roger the next morning at the Breakfast Club. I contacted him on his cell the night before, after I had finished with my business. Roger was already sitting at a table and had already ordered himself some food when I arrived. He spotted me when I entered and bid me over.

"Hey bro." I said with disdain.

"Coffee?" He asked.

"Sure." I answered.

Roger signalled for the waitress to bring me a cup of coffee. I drank it black.

"I can't see how you drink it like that." Roger remarked.

"You taught me to drink it black." I replied.

"Well, things were different then." He remarked.

"Yes they were" I agreed.

"So." Roger sipped his coffee. "I got a call from the Green Oak Township Police this morning."

"Really." I said in a monotone voice.

"It appears mom and dad's house burned down last night."

Roger spoke, awaiting some kind of reply from me.

"Shame" I said and sipped my coffee.

"I think you should leave town." Roger said matter of fact.

I looked him in the eye. "I was planning to leave, Bro. But now I want to stay just to piss you off."

"There's no need to be childish. You have what you came for. Now you can leave." Roger concluded. "I will send you a check for your part of the inheritance."

"No need." I said.

"That's ridiculous," He replied. "Of course you need it"

"I've seen what money does to people. I'd rather stay who I am" I smiled. "Thanks for the coffee. I stood and pushed my chair in. "Everyone dies, dear brother. But not everyone lives. Try to remember that." I turned and walked away, never looking back. That would be the last time I would hear from or see my brother, Roger.

Meredith was waiting in the parking lot for me, over by what used to be the smoke shop. Now it was something like a craft beer outlet or somesuch. I walked over to her and noticed a card under the driver's side windshield.

It read: Project: Delphi. It had writing at the bottom. "We're holding a place for you, Sorcerer".

"Of course you are, you bastards" I said to myself. I climbed into the driver's seat and took off on Grand River. I flipped the card into the wind as I drove. "I know how to find you." I said as the card flipped off into the wind. I took Grand River and got on I-96 headed west toward 23. I took 23 North. I had unfinished business to tend to. Unfinished business. Shit. This whole trip was about unfinished business.

I drove into nightfall. I closed my eyes and napped for a bit and left Meredith drive. I'm sure that scared the hell out of some truckers passing by. Maybe not. There's autonomous cars now, just none of them are 1974 Eldorado Cadillacs. I arrived at the Might Mac and tensed up as I crossed it. Just like I always had. Ever since I was a child, that bridge scared the shit out of me.

I paid the young lady at the toll booth. She wished me a safe trip. I wish there was some way for this trip to be safe.

Several hours more and I reached my final destination, Whitefish Point. I listened to the melodic cacophony of the sailors that had been claimed by Mother over the years. Her calm reassurance at my presence. I sat at the edge of her waters and began my communion.

"Mother. I need you to hold onto something for me." I said to Lake Superior. I reached into my pocket and produced the onyx shard that was once Esmarelda's tear. "She told me once she had never seen the Mother of All Lakes. Now that she is gone, I wanted to bring you a piece of her to hold on to." I clutched the onyx tightly. "Do you think you can do me that favor."

Lake Superior, in a rare moment of decorum, nodded yes with her waves. I cast the onyx into the crest. I stood, brushed the white sand off of my coat and pants and started back to the car. A cloud of blackflies parted in my path as if to let me know that my hard times were over, at least for the time being. I reached the Cadillac and sat in the passenger's seat.

I opened a newspaper that I had picked up at a roadside service station in Paradise. The headline read, "This Mean War!" Bullshit yellow journalism. Shit just put out there to get people worked up. I read the article. Unfortunately I had poorly estimated the nature of the world. I was so focused on saving mankind from some otherworldly force that I forgot about the thing man needed most saving from: itself. Maybe I didn't miss any of it. Maybe this is just karma catching up with me. I caught a pinprick of light in the side rear mirror. I focused on it until it became too intense to look at. Then in a second, everything was light as far as I could see.

"Looks like we lost, after all. Fuck it all. Why did we even do it?" I said to myself. I took note of the folded newspaper I threw down. A flyer from a local pizza joint fell out. Despite the apocalypse, there are apparently still pizza places. Maybe they'll also have Dippin' Dots.

"Merideth. Find me a place I can call home." I said to her. The engine started and settled into gear. Having completely expended my energies, I drifted off to sleep. Where the road would take me, I had no clue. But I knew that my days of adventuring were nowhere near finished. I had a whole world to unfuck. Yep, that's a word now.

Looks like we have a road trip ahead of us. It's been a good long while since I've had a proper road trip.

CPSIA information can be obtained
at www.ICGtesting.com
Printed in the USA
LVHW111400220920
666787LV00001B/207